There Was This Man Running

N.L. RAY

There Was This Man Running

MACMILLAN PUBLISHING CO., INC.
New York

Macmillan Publishing Co., Inc.
866 Third Avenue, New York, N.Y. 10022
Collier Macmillan Canada, Ltd.
First American edition 1981
Printed in the United States of America
10 9 8 7 6 5 4 3 2 1

LIBRARY OF CONGRESS CATALOGING IN PUBLICATION DATA
Ray, N   L
  There was this man running.
  SUMMARY: A storekeeper's family becomes unwittingly
involved with a mysterious, menacing being from outer
space.
  [1. Science fiction. 2. Extraterrestrial beings—
Fiction. 3. Kidnapping—Fiction] I. Title.
PZ7.R21016Th 1981 [Fic] 80-27225 ISBN 0-02-775760-9

For my Dear Sisters
and all the E's and G's

Contents

There Was This Man Running

Darren runs

"YOU'RE SURE YOU CAN HANDLE IT?" The managing director of the Australian branch of the James Eve Company looked searchingly at the young man seated opposite.

"Yes, Mr. Todd. We'll handle it." The other man nodded.

"They are only suspicions, but in view of the people involved—well, I wouldn't trust any of them. Two in particular. There's Bywater for one, I'd keep an eye on him. He could be working freelance or for one of our rivals. I hate to think what would happen if this new process got into the hands of our competitors!"

"And the other fellow?" Adam Spinks doodled in his notebook as he asked the question.

"Yes." The managing director hesitated. "I've nothing against him, nothing concrete that is, but he makes me uneasy. Name's O'Mara. Bill Jenkins, our sales manager, met him at a conference, and he's been hanging around a lot both here and out at the Works. Doesn't seem to have any occupation. Says he's an observer. Slides away from questions about his background. Smooth sort of guy."

"And your staff?"

"Loyal, as far as I know."

"O.K. Then we'll keep a watch on the ones you mentioned. I'll report through the usual channels. You know where to get hold of me if there are any new developments."

"Yes. Thanks." The two men shook hands and Adam left

the office. He drove off in a van with a crest on the door—three S's intertwined for SPINKS SECURITY SERVICE.

O'Mara would have enjoyed that conversation. No occupation or background? He had the appearance of a human male but was actually from another world. With his people he had inhabited a planet destroyed in a collision, the only survivors being those doing duty on a space platform that was now their only home. Powered by solar energy, it was large enough to be comfortable and to go wherever the Senior wished. The Senior had a great curiosity about the earth and its inhabitants, so each time the platform came within range, he sent observers to gather fresh facts. He was building up an interesting file on the primitive metallurgy used by humans.

This was to be his second visit to the planet Earth. Waiting for his briefing, O'Mara—the name he had chosen for this assignment—felt only a desire to get it over.

The Senior had addressed them all as they crowded together in the control room, then nodded toward O'Mara. "You've been before, you know what to do." He raised his voice. "Now remember the limits. If you don't return by Thakover, we can't wait for you. And if you lose your ank, you'll have to stay on Earth. We haven't the resources to run rescue operations."

O'Mara fingered the energy unit they called an ank. It locked into the flying suits and would also be the power source and means of communication. It was slightly convex, heavy, smooth, opaque.

The platform's carrier brought the research group within flying distance of Earth. O'Mara was first away. He pinpointed his target and dropped through the hatch. After he had landed, it did not take him long to build up the human body image he would inhabit during his stay. He had a great contempt for the human race; he could make them believe they saw just what he wanted them to see.

It was easy for him to gatecrash a conference at a large hotel, easier still to make a contact that would be useful. Bill Jenkins offered friendship, which O'Mara manipulated to his benefit. He had been alone in Jenkins's office using the ank to report to base when the man returned before he was expected. O'Mara quickly fumbled the ank toward the coin pocket of his trousers. A few hours later when he had a chance to finish his report, he discovered the ank was missing. He had a moment of blind panic. That was a mistake; it used too much power. He would have to find the ank. He just had to find it.

The caretaker of the building knew him and nodded as O'Mara came in through the basement entrance. Quickly he went upstairs. He was too late. The cleaners had been busy and the sales manager's office had already been done. He searched the floor, the desk, under cupboards. Nothing. He returned to the basement to the sacks of rubbish waiting to be disposed of. There was no flicker of response to his searching impulses.

A motorbike engine coughed and roared. O'Mara caught a spark of power as the rider went past him.

Darren ran down the stairs to the basement garage, whistling through his teeth. It had been so easy! The chick had done almost as he'd asked. The memory dot had been on the desk under the pad of the typewriter, though the silly chicken had put it on the left instead of the right side. It was safe now, along with the disc one of the cleaners had given him, in the box of matches he'd picked up from the sales manager's desk. His duties did not normally take him into the executive suite, but over the last few weeks, he'd been helping the female cleaners with any heavy work. The women liked his cheerful, cheeky face and didn't mind him following them around from room to room as they worked. Now, thinking about it, the lad clicked his heels together as he leaped from the last step to the floor.

"You're very cheerful tonight," the super said, grinning.

"Yeah. Well, why not? G'night Mist' Anderson."

" 'Night, Darren. Have a good holiday."

"Yeah, well, ta." Darren put on his helmet, started his machine and roared off, taillights and directional signals glowing in the gloom between the basement and the street. He rode masterfully, feeling the power under him, enjoying his control of it.

Until he was over the bridge and off the highway, he kept to the speed limit, but once he was on Ball's Head Road, his exhilaration needed an outlet. He opened the throttle and the cycle leaped forward.

The blue Crown was there, parked among the trees, but Darren circled the track once more before riding in beside it and cutting his motor. He walked across, helmet under his arm, and leaned one elbow on the door on the driver's side.

"O.K.?"

Darren nodded. Then his feeling of triumph overcame caution. "Piece of cake!" he smirked.

The man in the car held out his hand. Darren shook his head. "No way! I want to see the money first."

The interior light made Darren blink, but he looked eagerly at the bulky envelope on the seat. The man slid the flap open to show the fifty-dollar bills crammed inside but held it out of Darren's reach. "Well?" he said.

"Oh, don't worry, I've got it all right." Darren took a matchbox out of his pocket. "It's in here."

The lights of a car picked them out as it turned and gleamed on other cars parked on the grass off the roadway. They waited for it to go. Darren was pushing open the tray of the box with slow deliberation. The man in the car concealed his impatience, holding a cigarette to the dashboard lighter. He picked up the envelope once more and held it out.

Lights on high beam probed down the road, stopped. Darren looked round. "Cops!" he muttered uneasily, sighting the blue light. "Here, gimme." He reached toward the money as the patrol car came on again, and the man wrenched the matchbox out of his hand. The bike engine roared at the first kick and Darren was off up the road.

The patrol car stopped near the Crown and a cop sauntered over. "Got a light?" he asked, and was offered the glowing cigarette. "I'd prefer a match," the cop said and took the box out of the man's hand. He extracted a match, struck it, lit his cigarette and handed back the box. "Ta." He drew deeply and blew out a cloud of smoke. "Nice evening."

"Yes," said the man. "Isn't it?"

At home Darren read the message to call Linda. He hesitated, then dialed the number. "Darren," he said.

"Oh, Darren, I've been trying to get you for ages. Look, I couldn't do what you asked. . . ."

"Forget it."

"I'm sorry, I really am. I couldn't. . . ."

"Like I said, doll. Forget it."

"I'll see you . . . ?"

"Yeah, I'll be around." He hung up and shrugged his shoulders. He took out the money and held it near his face. It smelled rich. He folded the bills carefully and put them back in his pocket. "Gold Coast here I come," he crowed.

The man in the blue Crown waited until the patrol car had gone before he moved. He was still cold from the sweat that had broken out on his body when he'd been asked for his matches. It was a good thing the lad hadn't used an empty box! Silly young fool, darting off like that. Enough to make anyone suspicious. He tipped the matches out into his cupped palm. Nothing in the tray. He pushed his finger up into the cover, felt the tape and nodded to himself. Putting the matches back, he found something else—about the size of a penny, slightly convex, heavy, smooth, opaque. The man caught his breath, turning the thing over and over. What luck! Not only the process data but a sample! The kid could have asked for twice as much. The light glinted on the object in his hand. For a moment he thought he could see something in it, but when he looked closer, there was only the secretive, steely gray blueness of it. He transferred the two treasures into the place he had prepared.

There was no sound except an occasional laugh or the hoot of a ferry in the harbor. There was no wind stirring the trees, but suddenly, the man in the Crown felt a chill of unreasoning panic. The hair on the back of his neck bristled. He could feel, he swore he could feel, eyes boring into him out of the dark. For a fifty-year-long half minute he sat irresolute, unable to turn his head, smelling his own fear. Then he snapped off the light and started the car, driving without lights until he was on the roadway, and the powerful engine carried the car rapidly away. He reassured himself as he drove. He'd been careful to cover his tracks. His rivals could not have gotten on to him so quickly. Unless the young fool had been careless . . . .

Behind him a black Mercedes nosed out and followed.

Cass runs

STEWART MACKEN came round the corner full tilt and ran into Father O'Donovan. "Holy Mother!" gasped the priest, clinging to the boy and gyrating with him to preserve balance. "Cassowary Macken, d'ye have to go hell for leather at everything? Put me down now, don't hug the rest of the breath out of me!"

"I'm sorry, Father. I didn't expect you. Are you O.K.?" The boy steadied the frail old man.

"No thanks to you if I am, you red-headed rapscallion. Go easy now and don't be forever rushing everywhere. What's the hurry, is there a fire?"

The red-headed boy shook his head and regarded the priest with affection. "No, Father, not yet . . . I mean, not that I know of. Are you sure you're all right?"

Father O'Donovan fished in his pocket and slipped something into his mouth. "I'll eat you one day, I will so," he hissed.

Cass began to giggle, then broke into a full belly laugh. The priest sported a set of plastic vampire teeth and was contorting his face into horrid spasms. "Stop it, Father," he begged. "You're killing me!"

"Get off, then, and leave a poor old man alone. Is your mother well?"

"O.K., Father. Yes, she is, thanks. Sorry about the crash. See you." Cass was running again even as he spoke.

The priest watched him go, rubbing his middle and shaking his head. Going home to help in the shop, he thought. Just as well it wasn't the school case that had caught him!

Cass was still smiling. The Mackens weren't Catholics, but Father O'Donovan had been the parish priest since Creation, everyone knew him, and he knew all the older residents whether they were his flock or belonged to a friend of his Friend. He used to ride a bicycle with his hat on sideways, but age had caught up with him and he now rode the outer parish bounds in a Moke. It was no use trying to put on the dog with Father O'Donovan; he shamed people into being themselves.

The boy turned left from Florence Avenue into Harbor Street. Harbor Street went on between its blocks of flats and units, but Cass crossed over to where Wharf Road ran quietly before plunging downhill to the harbor. There was a glimpse of city skyline between the buildings, its feet in the water, its head in the clouds. Cass nodded to Mr. Vichelli, who was standing at the door of his greengrocery picking his teeth, and disappeared through the entrance of THE WHARF ROAD SUPERMARKET. It was no Woolworth's, but it served the area. Mr. Macken had done clever things for the high shelves with wire baskets that swung down on a steel slide to allow the customers to help themselves. It was a daily job for Cass to replenish the shelves against the homecoming rush of workers and school children. A bank of refrigerated cabinets ran along one wall of the shop.

Alanna Caterina looked up from the check-out where she was filing her nails. "Hi, brother," she called, and bent again to the task of perfecting the curve of her fingernail.

"Oh, hi," answered Cass. "Where's Mum?"

"Upstairs having a nap before Clare gets home. Could you

get me a carton of golden syrup before you start on the rest of the shelves? I can't lift it."

Cass laughed. "Oh, go on!" he said. "You don't have to kid me about your delicate femininity, you could pick up an elephant with one hand. What's the rush on golden syrup?"

"Some special recipe in the paper last night. Hurry up or we'll be swamped by the clamoring crowds."

"O.K., O.K. Are you going to try it?"

"Try what?"

"The recipe. It must be good if you expect such a rush."

"No chance. You can warn your stomach to start being disappointed; you'll be lucky to get ice cream and flavoring. Hurry, please, Cass."

Alanna Caterina helped Mrs. Macken in the shop. She was eighteen and waiting for her Romantic Dream to walk in to buy some caviar, be so struck by the raven-haired beauty at the check-out that he would drop the caviar, pick her up in strong arms and rush with her out to his Rolls—though a Bentley would do—and drive off to a luxurious penthouse complete with every labor-saving device ever invented.

"Can you bear up until I put my jeans on?" Cass didn't wait for an answer but crashed up the stairs, tripping over Seville asleep in the darkest corner. The cat yowled and re-treated. "Silly boofhead!" shouted Cass. "I might have got killed!"

"Is that you, Cass?"

Cass stood still, ashamed. "Yes, Mum. Gee, did I wake you up? I'm sorry. I fell over Seville."

"Not to worry, it's time I was up. I thought it might have been an invasion from outer space when I heard the row."

"Oh, Mum!" Cass laughed as he changed his clothes. His mother came and stood at the door, smiling at him. Her hair was snowy white, curling over her head in tight ringlets, which made it look as if she wore a helmet. Under the close-cropped hair, her face and eyes were young. "School O.K., son?"

"Not bad. I nearly knocked down Father O'Donovan on the way home, and he put in his vampire teeth and threatened . . . ."

"CA-ASS? GOLDEN SYRUP, REMEMBER?"

"Oh, blast! I'll tell you later, Mum." Cass gave his mother a hug as he went past her and shot down the stairs and out to the storeroom. He loaded the golden syrup onto a trolley and pulled it out into the shop. Expertly he built a pyramid of it on the "Special" table where it would catch the eye of impulse buyers.

"What's it called, this pudding?"

"Tickytacky Yumyum."

"You're joking!"

"No, honest. That's what it's called. Why?"

"Aw, nothing." Cass retreated with his trolley but came back soon after with a piece of cardboard that he arranged in the display. ARE YOU HAVING TICKYTACKY YUMYUM TO-NIGHT? was spread out in large letters across the board. "That should sell a few," Cass said proudly. "Where's this rush you're talking about?" He glanced through the window. "Here comes Mrs. Leadbetter," he warned and disappeared into the storeroom.

" 'Lo 'lanna. Hot, ain't it?"

"Hello, Mrs. Leadbetter. Are you feeling it, then?"

Mrs. Leadbetter fanned herself. She was contained in a bright floral dress, and Alanna found herself wondering what happened when Mrs. Leadbetter took it off. Did her abundance overflow in all directions?

"What's new, then? What's this?" She studied the placard

in the heap of golden syrup tins. " 'Are you having Tickytacky Yumyum tonight?' " she read out in a flat voice. "I
suppose your young brother did that. He's spoiled rotten. I
said it to Art only last night. 'That young Macken boy is
spoiled rotten,' I said."

"Do you think so?" Alanna's voice was sweet.

In the storeroom, the listening Cass grew hot. Silly old cow,
he thought. He felt like shouting out something rude, pre-
tending he did not know she was in the shop. That would
fix her! "Be nice to all the customers," he could hear his
mother's voice clearly in his mind. Cass sighed. It was his red
hair, he supposed. He got mad so easily.

The shop was filling up with customers. Cass went about his
work of restocking the fixtures, putting prices on new stock
and answering his sister's demands. His mother was back in
the delicatessen section slicing Devon or pressed ham, wrapping dairy foods and waiting for children to choose sweets
and popsicles.

Cass heard the bus start off from outside and looked up in
time to see Clare come through the door. She stopped short
when she saw the placard. Putting down her bag, she picked
up a felt pen from her sister's desk and began to draw beside
the lettering. In no time she had sketched a family seated
round a table, cleaned-up dessert plates in front of them,
beaming smiles on all faces.

"YOU'RE A CLEVER PUSS!" Mrs. Leadbetter's shout could be
heard in Bondi.

Everyone in the shop jumped. Cass frowned. No matter
how often they told Mrs. Leadbetter not to shout at Clare,
she never heeded. The smile on Clare's face vanished as she
put her hand up to her hearing aid. Cass came past her with
an empty carton and touched her arm. She turned instantly
and followed him out to the storeroom.

"Poor little beggar. Isn't she a poor little beggar, Mrs. Macken?"

Clare's mother bit her lip and went on slicing ham. Then she looked up and smiled at Mrs. Leadbetter. "Who, Clare? She's fine!" she said firmly.

Everyone knew that Clare had been born with defective hearing because of German measles, but Mrs. Leadbetter was the only one who shouted about it. She was convinced that no hearing device worked efficiently enough to pick up a normal tone of voice and always doubled her decibel output when speaking to Clare.

"She's our cross," Mrs. Macken often said when Mrs. Leadbetter was being discussed.

"She's not bad at heart," Alanna Caterina reminded them. "Just insensitive. I rather like her."

"She stinks!"

"Cass! Don't ever let me hear you say that about anyone. It's not your place to comment on a customer's hygiene."

"O.K., Mum, keep your hair on. I didn't mean she *stinks*, I just mean she stinks."

"She scares me." Clare's uncertain voice broke in before her mother could say any more to Cass. "She sees so much."

They all stared at Clare, who nodded at them and repeated the words. "She sees so *much*."

"What do you mean, Clare?"

"She looks at you as if she knows what you're thinking. Haven't you noticed?"

"She'd get more than she bargained for if she looked in my mind!"

"That'll do, Stewart." Mr. Macken put an end to the conversation.

Now, in the storeroom, Cass looked at his younger sister. Her fair hair was drawn tightly back from her head and done in a little plait. Her eyes were blue gray, whereas Alanna's were deep blue. Clare was like a candle in the dark, thought Cass, and Alanna was a blazing neon sign. "Take no notice of the old hippopotamus," he said.

Clare smiled. "Your aura's getting dark," she answered.

"O.K., but I can't help getting mad at her." Cass kicked a pile of empty cartons. Clare began to stack them, small ones inside bigger ones, with quick, neat movements. Mrs. Macken came in and Clare looked up immediately. You'd never know she was deaf, Cass thought, she seemed to sense movement.

"Dad's home," their mother said. "Are you ready, Clare?"

Clare nodded. She sketched an arc above her brother's head with one hand and said, "Keep it pale, Mack."

"Oh, you!" Cass retorted. He worked on, aware of the increased tempo in the shop, yet thinking about his mother and sister upstairs working away at tone and pitch so that Clare's voice would sound normal. It was tiring work, stretching patience on both sides, but Clare was eager to master more words. Mr. Macken had just bought Clare a color-sound transducer that allowed deaf people to see their speech and correct areas of tonal flatness.

"Stewart."

"Yes, Dad?" Cass straightened up. Alone of the family, Mr. Macken never used his son's nickname. There were four Stewarts in Cass's class at school and two of them had the same surname. The other boys started teasing and soon were chanting:

> *"What do you do with the toughest meat?*
> *You Stewart, Stewart, Stewart!"*

From there it was only a step to Irish, Steak and Kidley, Casserole and Ditto. The Ditto Stewart was named Stewart Stuart. Father O'Donovan insisted on calling Cass "Cassowary" because he didn't like red peppers in his stew, he said.

Mr. Macken was tall and broad shouldered with a fringe of faded gingery hair clinging to the slopes of his bald skull. His eyes were the same color as Alanna's. He gestured back toward the shop. "Got any more golden syrup, son? There's a lot of Tickytacky being served up tonight."

"I think the least Alanna can do is make some for us, don't you, Dad?"

"You don't want your gut gummed up with that muck, do you?"

The desire to laugh with his father fought with Cass's stomach. "I wouldn't mind," he admitted. "Just to try it."

"Do you want a hand?"

"No, thanks, Dad. I'll put out half a dozen. It's not long to closing. Will it be O.K. if I clean up in the morning? I'll get up early and do it."

"I'll help you. Thank goodness it's only a half day, eh?"

"Corned beef, please, Dad!" Alanna's call was frantic.

"Coming." Mr. Macken turned and strode off, Cass following with the golden syrup.

"Tickytacky Yumyum here I come come," chanted Cass. "Sticky up your tumtum, rumtum, tiddlyum . . . ouch!"

Alanna Caterina smiled as her fingers flew over the cash register keys. She could kick sideways like a cow, as Cass's shin had just found out.

The man runs

THE MAN WAS RUNNING when he got to Florence Avenue. There was no sign of pursuit. Perhaps he had shaken them off. The Crown had run out of petrol after a game of hide-and-seek with the following car, and he'd abandoned it and been dodging round corners, through lanes, backtracking, but always forced toward the water. It was as though they could read his mind and cut off his retreat every time. Just a glimpse of the black Mercedes was enough to make his heart jump and his nerves tangle in the pit of his stomach. It seemed to be there whenever he turned a corner. They *must* have been watching him. He turned into Harbor Street gasping for breath. The ferry! There'd be a ferry doing its first run. If he hurried . . . .

Cass and his father were in the small yard at the side of the shop, stacking empty cartons. The early morning still smelled fresh, birds were calling *peta peta peta* from the trees in the street, daring the ginger tom who was busy washing a hind leg and paying no attention to them. The sound of a trawler came up the hill from the harbor, its fussy hurrying engine note carrying in the clear air. A train on the bridge shouted its approach and grumbled away. A truck labored up the hill. Cass sniffed. He loved the smells of the city—petrol, diesel, trains, people. He wouldn't live anywhere else for all the money in the world.

"There, you can take that lot round to Vichelli's, he'll be glad of them for his orders, Stewart. Stewart!"

"Sorry, Dad. I was just thinking."

"What with?" The twinkle in his father's eye softened the sarcasm. "Come on, get these out of the way and we'll go in for breakfast."

Cass unlatched the gate opening onto the street. He paused, listening. "Someone's in a hurry."

Mr. Macken came and stood behind his son. Seville stopped washing himself, one leg stuck out awkwardly. A man came running toward them, swaying a little, red in the face with effort, mouth wide open. He had nearly reached them when he fell. Cass couldn't make himself move. He stared at the awkward heap on the footpath, feeling foolish. Mr. Macken brushed past him and knelt down, turning the man gently onto his back.

"Just stay with him, son. I think it's his heart. I'll get the ambulance. Don't move him."

"Righto." Cass squatted down beside the man. A bit fat to be running so fast, no wonder he keeled over. His expensive suit was marked with water where Mr. Vichelli had hosed down the front of his shop and footpath. Cass brushed at it, wondering should he be doing something more useful. The man opened his eyes and Cass stared straight into them before he realized. They were pale gray, frightened, questioning. Cass could smell the fear on the man. You could tell a lot about a person by smell. The man moved. "Just take it easy," Cass soothed. "Dad's ringing the ambulance. Just lie quiet."

"Don't—don't let . . . ."

"Stay quiet, mister. Don't wear yourself out." Cass watched in horror as the blood drained out of the man's face and left it the color of putty. He could hear his mother calling out that she was bringing a pillow and a blanket.

The man made another effort to move. He raised his hand and held it out toward Cass. The clenched fingers opened. "Take . . . for me. I'll . . . come back . . . get it. Don't . . . don't let them . . . don't tell . . . ." The voice faded. Cass looked at the key ring, nodded, and put it in his pocket. Was this the ambulance? They had been quick! But it wasn't, just a black Mercedes coming slowly round the corner, two men in the front. It checked for a moment then ran smoothly past and turned into Florence Avenue as Mrs. Macken hurried out.

"Can I be of any help?"

Cass jerked round, nearly losing his balance. He hadn't heard anyone coming. Mrs. Macken answered, "Not unless you're a doctor. We're waiting for the ambulance now and thought we'd better not move him. Are you a doctor?"

"No. Would you like me to stay?"

Cass stood up. "We'll manage, thanks. Don't want to delay you."

The young man nodded, looked hard at them, and walked off.

"I haven't seen him before, Mum, have you?"

"No, I don't think I have, Cass. But you know how it is, there are always new people coming into the flats and units around here, and they all move on a Saturday. Cass, go and turn the gas down under the kettle, will you please? Make the tea if it's boiling."

"Will you be O.K.?"

"Of course! Anyway, here comes Mr. Vichelli. Morning, Mr. Vichelli, lovely day?"

Cass sprinted inside, narrowly missing a collision with his father at the gate. "What's going on out there?" It was Alanna Caterina, yawning at the top of the stairs.

"There was this man running down the footpath, had a

heart attack or something. Why don't you get dressed and go and hold his hand? He looks rich."

"Big deal!"

Cass laughed, looking up at his sister. She was beautiful even in her old cotton dressing gown with her hair all messed about. " 'O Alanna Caterina! You're so beautiful I could eat you! You are a sugarplum, sweet on the lips and bitter on the tongue!' " Cass mimicked his sister's latest boy friend.

"Shut up, little boy. Little *red-headed* boy. And get on with your jobs."

Cass made a rude noise and disappeared into the kitchen where the kettle was boiling angrily. He made the tea and put the cozy over the pot. Clare came in. Cass made signs of drinking and pointed to the teapot. Clare nodded and began putting cups on the table. The Saturday morning routine went on. There would hardly be a chance to draw breath from when the shop opened until closing time.

Over breakfast, they talked about the incident. "Did you know the man, Dad?"

"No, Alanna. I haven't seen him around here. Mid-forties, well dressed, solid build, brown hair a bit thin, gray eyes—I think they were gray."

Cass nodded. "That's right. Very pale gray. Very frightened."

"You might be frightened, too, if you were having a heart attack."

"He was scared rotten, I tell you. I could smell him."

"Cass! How often do I have to tell you . . . ."

Clare broke in. "He is a very smelly boy, Mum. It's a wonder he turned out to be a boy, he might have been a bloodhound!"

Cass grinned at her. "Thank you, Lady Clare, for those kind words. I can't help it if my nose has talent!"

THE MAN RUNS 19

"I suppose he will have papers with him that will tell who he is. It will be a shock for his family. Perhaps we should have . . . ?"

"The hospital will fix that," Mr. Macken said. "Don't worry, Mother. We did all we could for him."

Cass looked up, opened his mouth, then shut it. "Don't tell," the man had said. He felt Clare's eyes on him and grinned at her. It would be hard keeping a secret from Clare.

Mrs. Macken did not work in the shop on Saturdays. Mr. Macken, who worked with machines all week, said it did him good to get among people. When he opened the shop, Mr. Vichelli strolled along from next door and leaned against the wall admiring Alanna Caterina. He had tried so hard to get her for his son, but young people had no respect these days. The girl had said no, thanks, but his son had laughed at him for being old-fashioned enough to think of an arranged marriage. "Did you find out who he was?" Mr. Vichelli asked.

"Who who was?" Alanna Caterina arranged the change in the drawer of the cash register.

"The feller this morning. Your momma was looking after him. He didn't look too good."

"He wasn't well enough to give his name," Alanna Caterina said cruelly.

"Did the ambulance say where they were taking him?" Mr. Vichelli persisted.

"Try the mater." Mr. Macken winked at his daughter. "If you really want to know."

Mr. Vichelli always wanted to know. "I wonder why he was running?" he went on. "At that hour of the day. Doesn't live around here."

"Could have been running for the ferry," Cass remarked. "He'd have just made the early one if he hadn't fallen down."

"For a minute I thought that black Merc was going to stop

and pick him up." Mr. Vichelli was frowning, remembering the scene.

"You saw it, too, did you? Two fellers in the front."

"Only one," Mr. Vichelli stated with conviction. Cass was going to argue but his father shook his head at him.

"Probably been out all night and running home to his wife," Alanna Caterina suggested.

Mr. Vichelli shrugged and hitched his trousers. That girl! He wondered if she teased him on purpose. "I gotta go. If you hear anything . . . ."

"We'll let you know." It was a chorus from the Mackens. Mr. Vichelli always liked to know what was going on.

Mrs. Leadbetter arrived, displacing peace like a sonic boom. "I've just heard!" she announced breathlessly. "I slept in. Why didn't you send for me? I've got me St. John's certificate. I'da come, you know that."

"I'm sure you would, Mrs. Leadbetter. More like St. Peter he needed, poor coot."

"I coulda given him heart massage, or mouth-to-mouth. I learned it all."

Cass had a vision of Mrs. Leadbetter blotting out her patient with her abundance and retired to the storeroom giggling. He tried to stop but only succeeded in turning a giggle into a snort.

"You've got your trials, poor souls," Mrs. Leadbetter's voice went on. "As if Clare wasn't enough. What's wrong with that boy, Mr. Macken?"

"Not much that I know of," Mr. Macken replied. "Stewart!"

"Yes, Dad?" Cass came into the shop, scarlet faced.

"Carry Mrs. Leadbetter's groceries home for her, will you?"

"But I haven't . . . ." Cass began.

"Stewart will tell you all about it, Mrs. Leadbetter. He was there this morning."

"Oh, no, Dad!" Cass glanced from his father to his sister. They looked smug. Mrs. Leadbetter hesitated, then followed. She lived in the top story of a terrace across the road and made Cass go up the stairs in front of her. The wood groaned and creaked as Mrs. Leadbetter ascended and Cass kept expecting to crash down in a flurry of splintering timber.

"Put them on the kitchen table. Now what about a cool drink? Sit down and tell me what happened."

"I'd better be getting back, there's a lot to do." Cass could hear the birds in Mr. Leadbetter's aviary and his voice talking to them.

"Oh, go on! Five minutes won't hurt you. Your dad said you were to tell me. There's some Chester Cake too. Now tell me."

Cass felt the saliva run into his mouth. Chester Cake! It wasn't fair, the temptation was too great. By the time he had eaten it and drunk his glass of soda, Mrs. Leadbetter had drained him of information. He eyed the last piece of cake on the plate, trying not to want it. Mrs. Leadbetter pushed it toward him. "Take it with you," she said.

"Thanks. Well, bye now." Cass ran down the stairs, glad to get away. He nibbled a corner of the Chester Cake and then remembered that Clare liked it too. He nibbled the other three corners to make it look even and wrapped it up in his handkerchief.

Father O'Donovan drove past in his Moke. When he saw Cass, he blew the horn, then took both hands off the wheel and waggled them in his ears and poked out his tongue. Cass waved, laughing. The old man needed a team of guardian angels, he thought.

The Saturday morning ran its usual hectic course. They were all pleased when the clearing up was done and the shop locked for the weekend.

Saturday night sing-in

ON THE WAY HOME from the beach that afternoon, Mr.
Macken stopped at the hospital. "I might just go in and see
how our friend is," he said.

"I'll come with you," Cass offered.

"We'll wait in the car, dear. They might not let you see
him anyway."

"Always a possibility, Mother. Whichever way it goes, we
won't be long. Come on, Stewart."

Reception was helpful. "Mr. Bywater is popular. There
have been quite a few inquiries. Are you relatives?"

"No. He collapsed outside our shop and we thought we'd
find out how he was."

"You can't see him, I'm afraid. He's in intensive care. Perhaps in a few days?"

"Thank you. I'm sure he's getting every attention. Come
along, Stewart."

Cass followed his father out. His nose had been working
overtime taking in the hospital smells—floor polish, antiseptic,
suffering. He hoped he'd never have to go into the hospital
except as a visitor.

There was a rush on the bathroom when they got home,
Mrs. Macken claiming it first because she had to get the meal.
Alanna Caterina said she had to wash her hair, so she must
be next, and Cass volunteered not to have a shower at all if

it would be any help. Clare walked up to him and sniffed at him, shaking her head. She pinched her nose between two fingers and backed away, waving her arm about as if to ward off something nasty.

"Looks as if you'd better, Stewart. If you're quick you can go before Clare."

Cass laughed. Clare went to help her mother in the kitchen. She loved Saturday nights. Once the shop was closed on Saturday, the whole family went out. Warm afternoons were spent at the beach, others exploring Sydney's new suburbs, or walking through bushland. Sometimes Alanna Caterina spent the time with a friend. Mrs. Macken did the washing and house cleaning on Saturday morning while her husband took her place in the shop. There were usually extra people for the evening meal, and afterward they had a sing-in. Alanna Caterina's current boyfriend was always invited. She said it gave her a chance to see him in a family situation and was a good test of character. Mr. and Mrs. Vichelli never missed, Mrs. Vichelli bringing a pizza of enormous proportions and delicious content and a fruit salad made from shop stock that wouldn't keep over until Monday.

Cass, fresh from the shower, took over in the kitchen and watched his mother making scones. She was so quick. She added a little sugar and two tablespoons of powdered milk to the flour, melted the butter, added the milk and mixed it quickly into the dry ingredients with a knife. The dough was kneaded on the floured board until it was elastic, then patted to an even thickness and cut with a baby-food tin with both ends out. Deftly, Mrs. Macken glazed the scones with milk and then arranged them on the hot tray, sprinkled with flour.

"Hop down and get some jam, Cass, please. What would you like tonight?"

"Blackberry?"

"Everyone likes blackberry. All right. It never lasts, that's the only trouble."

"Nothing does, Mum. That's what our teacher says. 'Nothing lasts, thank God,' he says."

Mrs. Macken laughed. "Is he thankful that his pleasures are fleeting, too?"

"I dunno, Mum. He always says it about troubles. I'll ask him."

"You'd better be careful. He might take a dim view."

"Oh, he's all right, really. Who's coming tonight, Mum?"

"The Vichellis, of course."

"Of course! We couldn't do without Mrs. Vichelli's violin and Mr. Vichelli's glorious 'Come Back to Sorrento' tenor!"

"And Vincent and Trevor and Father O'Donovan, I think."

"Yuk! Alanna Caterina sure gets some funny fellers. That Vincent . . . ."

"On your way, garbage. No one asked you to give my friends the O.K."

"Help!" yelled Cass in mock terror as Alanna Caterina advanced on him. "I go, I go! Don't hit me, Alanna Caterina my little sugarplum! Preserve your peaceful aura and be ki-ind to me." Cass skidded out of the kitchen and down the stairs to the shop, helped by a packet of breakfast food hurled at him by his sister. He found the blackberry jam and returned whistling, putting his head round the door to see if he could safely venture back.

Conversation round the meal table was lively. Cass sat opposite Clare and watched to see that she did not miss anything. Clare found her hearing aid confusing in a crowd, turning it off and relying on her lip reading and hands. She did not speak much.

Vincent and Trevor, sitting on either side of Alanna Caterina, eyed each other warily.

"Where's Caramello tonight, Mr. Vichelli?"

The greengrocer rolled his eyes. "That boy? He's gone to the dogs."

"Oh, I am sorry!" Alanna Caterina looked sympathetic. "You'd wonder how he could, with such a good family influence as you and Mrs. Vichelli behind him. Do you think it is too late to rehabilitate him?"

Cass was watching his mother. She was frowning but trying to stifle her laughter at the same time. For all his years in Australia, Mr. Vichelli still had trouble with the English idiom and Alanna Caterina was forever teasing him.

"No, no, he is not going down the drain, the dogs, Harold Park!" Mrs. Vichelli broke in. Her eyes were full of mischief. She did not mind Mr. Vichelli being teased among friends. He had not even noticed that Alanna had put an extra syllable in Carmelo's name.

Mr. Vichelli was not without his revenge. "And which one of these is to be your lucky husband?" he asked Alanna, nodding at her swains.

" 'The palace denies the rumor,' " Alanna Caterina laughed. "We're just friends, aren't we, guys?"

The guys looked uneasy.

"Bring out the hat," Mrs. Macken said. "Let's get this cleared up and then on with the music." An ancient top hat that Grandfather Macken had worn to his wedding was produced from a cupboard and slips of paper put into it. There was one for each person. Father O'Donovan stirred them and then took the hat round, inviting everyone to take a dip. All but three of the slips were blank; the others contained a single word: *CLEAR   WASH   WIPE.*

Vincent drew *CLEAR*. He had been to a Saturday evening before and knew what to do. Clare and Cass drew the washing up. Vincent had the table empty in double quick time, jealous of every moment Trevor was left with Alanna Caterina. Mrs. Vichelli began to tune her violin.

"Oh, hurry, Cass."

"Stand clear," said Cass. He filled the sink with hot water and began sloshing crockery onto the drainer. "Hey, listen to Dad, he's really going to town on the squeeze box tonight!" Clare nodded. She wiped plates and stacked them away, giving an extra rub in places where Cass's speed had interfered with his efficiency.

"Do you need a hand, Cassowary?"

Cass spun round. Father O'Donovan peered in the door, tapping a comb in the palm of his hand. "No, thanks, Father. We'll be there soon. Don't let them start without us."

"What will I do, throw a fit?"

"You'll think of something!"

"Too late." The old priest withdrew his head and Cass heard him join in with his light baritone as the first song of the evening began. Clare shut the cupboard door on the last of the saucepans and waited for Cass to wipe down the sink. They went into the sitting room together and found themselves a space on the floor.

It wasn't that they were so good, Cass thought, just that they had so much fun. Mrs. Vichelli played her violin, putting in her own variations, Mr. Macken had an ancient and much-treasured concertina with a couple of stops missing, his wife switched from recorder to tin whistle, Father O'Donovan played the comb with some flair, and more rarely, the jew's-harp. Sometimes they all stopped playing and just sang. Alanna's contralto and Mr. Vichelli's tenor made pleasant harmonies; Mr. Macken added his bass and the children their soprano. Nobody minded that Clare's voice wandered from the note. Vincent had brought his guitar, which he was learning to play, but always seemed to find the right chord when the singers were two bars ahead of him. After a while, he abandoned it and got himself a boiler and a couple of wooden spoons from the kitchen and did a solo drum turn. Not to be outdone, Trevor showed his gymnastic ability by throwing his body around in one spot like an octopus with fleas. Clare watched, fascinated, as he finally sank down at Alanna's feet. Cruelly, Alanna dropped a carnation on his perspiring face and shouted "Encore!"

"May I come in?" No one had heard the knock. "I put the chain on as you said."

Mrs. Macken got up. "Hello there, come in. Can you hear yourself think in all this din? Come and meet the others."

The young man who came into the room was fair haired, of medium height, with calm, twinkly brown eyes. He smiled and waited for Mrs. Macken to introduce him. "Father O'Donovan, do you know Peter Graham? He's the new man at St. Margaret's."

"How's the fishing?" the old man asked, extending his hand.

"They're only nibbling at the bait yet, but there are plenty in the pool. I'll get you to bless the hook for me."

After the introductions there was a strained silence. Peter looked at Vincent's guitar. "May I?"

"Sure, sure. You might be better than I am."

"Couldn't be much worse," muttered Trevor. The chords were strong and clear. Soon everyone was singing. Clare got up from the floor and climbed onto her father's knee. She leaned against his chest, one hand on his neck feeling the music coming out of him. She had turned off her hearing aid; it made her tired when there was a confusion of noise. Mr.

Macken cradled her gently and Clare felt the warmth of his love surrounding her.

Peter broke away into a yodeling song that had everyone cheering and clapping. His face was alight with laughter as he finished. "Sing this one with me," he said. "It goes like this: *'We are heirs of the Father, we are joint heirs with the Son, we are children of the Kingdom, we are family, we are one.'* I'll sing it through first." They sang it three times and clamored for more. The evening went on from song to song, classical, jazz, chorus, country and western. By suppertime, Cass was dry but elated. It had been a really great night.

" *'Let the earth rejoice and everybody sing,'* " he caroled as he carried in the scones.

" *'Praise God, praise God for His wonderful love,'* " Peter finished for him. He took a bite of scone. "Better praise God for Mrs. Macken's scones, too!" He raised his cup in the direction of his hostess.

"If you'd made them as often as I have," she laughed, "you'd be a dab hand at them too."

Clare was asleep, leaning against her father's chair. Cass went over to her and blew gently on her cheek. She opened her eyes and smiled at him. Cass put his hands on his cheek and bent his head. She nodded, got up and went out with him. At the door she turned. "Good night," she said.

Later, when Cass went into her room, she was in bed but not asleep. He sat down and grinned at her. "Tired?"

"Happy. I like that Peter, don't you? He has a very steady aura. A bit like Mum's, but hers is paler, more gold color."

Cass nodded, touched her hand and left her. At the door, he turned out the light. Funny, dear little kid, he thought, seeing auras. He had tried but couldn't. When she drew people, there was always a surrounding color. Mrs. Macken's was golden orange, Alanna's yellow, that of Mr. Macken and Cass pale green (but Cass's went dark when he was angry, she said), and Father O'Donovan's was like a rainbow, with shifting colors. Clare judged all her contacts by the electrical impulses their bodies threw out; she said it was her cat's whiskers. "Like your nose, only different," she told her brother.

Now where had he put the key ring? Cass threw off the bedclothes and then decided not to bother. It was in the pocket of his jeans in the clothes basket in the bathroom. Safe enough until morning. He could see it in his mind—a brass button with a raised railway engine on the convex side of it, an old-fashioned engine, and on the back + *C. J. Webb & Co Ltd + London.* There were three keys on the split ring that hung from the button shank. One was a car key; the others looked like door keys, quite ordinary door keys. What had the feller meant—"Don't let them . . . don't tell . . ."? Who were *they* and "don't tell" *what?* Mr. Bywater had been running; he had been frightened.

Cass yawned. It had been a long day.

A stubborn coot of a cat

"VICHELLI'S WAS BROKEN INTO last night." Mr. Macken replaced the phone as he spoke.

Mrs. Macken looked up, horrified. "While they were up here with us?"

"Must have been. We were kicking up enough racket in here; we'd never have heard a thing."

"Is anything missing?"

"They can't tell. Mrs. Vichelli said all their clothes were thrown onto the floor, things tipped over, but nothing taken that they know of. They didn't like to bother us last night."

"Did they take the color telly?" Cass asked.

"No, not even the color telly. They had the change for Monday with them, of course."

"Are they getting the cops?"

"Yes, they've been and gone."

"Why do I have to miss out on all the exciting things?"

"Serve you right for sleeping in. Go and wake Alanna, please, Cass."

"No need," said Alanna, coming in. "What's going on?"

"Vichelli's was broken into last night."

"Good grief!" Alanna Caterina sipped orange juice. "They'll get a dog now, for sure. They've been threatening to. That will shake up your precious cat, Cass."

Cass laughed. "Seville is a match for any dog," he said. "Has

31

anyone seen him this morning, by the way?" No one had.
"I'll just go and see if he's in the yard."

"Excuse yourself!"

"Sorry, Mum. May I be excused, please?"

"Off you go."

Cass hurried. He was back within minutes. "Dad, have you
seen our yard?"

"Perhaps it went off with your cat," Alanna said lazily.

"Isn't it there, Stewart?"

"It's no joke, and you can shut up, Alanna! Dad, someone's
been in our yard too. It's a mess."

Mr. Macken got up so quickly his chair fell over. He did
not wait to pick it up but rushed down the stairs. Cartons
and paper were strewn all over the yard, a packet of washing
powder tipped over in the laundry, cupboards cleared out
and contents left all anyhow and Seville's basket torn in half.
Cass made a move to straighten things, but his father said,
"Don't touch things, Stewart, just leave them as they are. I'll
ring the police."

"You'd better get yourself ready for Sunday School, Cass."

"Not today, Mum! Can't I wait for the cops to come?"

"You certainly may not. Hurry up." Mrs. Macken lowered
her voice. "I want Clare out of here, Cass."

Cass hesitated. "O.K., Mum. Look, I haven't found Seville
yet. Keep an eye out for him will you? His bed's all busted."

"He can look out for himself. Don't worry."

Cass dived into the laundry basket in the bathroom and
found his jeans. The key ring was still in the pocket. He
transferred it to the pocket of the pants he was wearing and
went to find Clare.

All through Sunday School, Cass was restless and inatten-
tive. He kept wondering what was happening at home. Clare

came up to him afterward with a sample of the chocolate crackles her class had made and offered it to Cass.

"Sure you don't want it? Thanks." He stuffed it into his mouth. "Look, there's Mum." He raced across to meet Mrs. Macken. "Did they find anything, Mum? Have they been?"

"They'd tried to get in the side door, but apart from that, nothing. Where's Clare? Oh, I see." She walked across to where Clare was waiting. "Dad's stayed to clean up the yard, so he's not coming. Let's go in."

"Any sign of Seville?"

"Yes, I forgot. He's O.K. except he's up a tree and won't come down. He might come down for you."

Cass went into church prepared to be bored. He hated the salad hymn sandwiches with so much "let us" in all the words that he was always tempted to ask for the mayonnaise. He got a shock. Peter Graham's ideas on worship were anything but dull. Cass found himself joining in the happenings and even listening to the sermon. He felt a bit doubtful about whether it was right to play the guitar in church, but the choruses were so joyful and the praise so sincere, perhaps it was O.K. Even when Peter had first the children, then anyone who felt like it, marching up one aisle and down the other, all singing while he played the guitar and led them, it was somehow holy.

After the service, there was a lot of talk among the congregation. Some liked it, others hated it, but the children were enthusiastic. "It's got life, man," one boy told the preacher as he shook hands. "I'm coming again!"

"Well, Cass?" Mrs. Macken asked the question after a very silent walk.

"I dunno, Mum. I enjoyed it, it was different, but I was a bit shocked, too."

"You didn't get time to be bored, did you?"

"That's for sure! What about you, Clare, did you like it?"

Clare looked from her mother to her brother, smiled and nodded. She was so happy she couldn't tell whether she walked or floated. The I AM of God surrounded her and she loved the whole world.

Mr. Macken had the yard and laundry cleaned up, but Seville was still at the top of the tree. Cass went out into the street and called him. Seville peered through the leaves and answered with his unmusical *miaow* but would not come down. Mrs. Macken came out. "Get your dinner, son. You can try him with some meat later."

Cass went upstairs with her, but Mr. Macken said he'd already tried him with meat. "And milk. Even opened a tin of sardines, but he won't budge for me. Must have had a fright. He'll come down when he's hungry, but the way he's fed, it might take a week."

"Oh, Dad, you are heartless!"

"Not a bit. If he got up, he can get down."

"Sometimes people have to get the fire brigade to get cats down off poles," Alanna Caterina said solemnly. "I suppose they must charge for it. Hey, Cass, perhaps you could set fire to the tree, and then they'd have to come and put it out."

"Huh." Cass was not impressed. "Try your good ideas on Trevor; he might be more open to suggestion."

After dinner, Cass eased himself out of a window onto the iron roof of the shop verandah and reached inside for Seville's plate of food. The cat was facing down, clinging to the tree trunk, tail lashing. "Puss puss. Come on, Seville. Come on, puss. Look, it's your favorite food." Cass held up the plate and waved it around. Seville yowled plaintively. Cass sat down and pulled himself along the iron on his bottom, using his legs as a lever until he reached the low parapet that ran around the shop area. His foot kicked against something and he saw it was a tennis ball. It rolled further along the gutter.

Seville wanted to get down. He'd been treed for too long; he was hungry, indignant and martyred. Cass understood all this from Seville's tone of voice. He made soothing noises in reply and coaxed and encouraged Seville from limb to limb. It took a long time. Finally the cat stopped short on a thin branch that was nearly within reach. Cass straddled the parapet and held out his arm as far as it would go. Seville stretched toward him, then retreated. Cass's patience snapped. "You silly mongrel cat!" he roared. "Wasting my afternoon. Come on!" He leaned farther out and lost his balance. With a yell of fury, he grabbed at the tree as he fell, and Seville leaped across him onto the roof, where he ran straight to his dish and began eating.

"Of all the rotten ungrateful sods of misbegotten misery!" Cass was still yelling as he bumped through the foliage, wildly trying to grasp a branch thick enough to hold him, and succeeding only in breaking off bunches of leaves. With a final screech of vituperation, he hit the roadway and lay still, the greenery quivering around him.

"I'M COMING! I'M COMING! DON'T MOVE!" It was Mrs. Leadbetter, racing down the steps from her house to the footpath in a series of jarring leaps. The impetus was too much for her and she crossed the road half-hopping, half-running, and flopped down beside Cass. He was getting his wind back and opened his eyes to find her huge bulk looming over him.

"HELP!" His terror was quite unreasoning as he rolled out of reach, scrambled to his feet and bolted round the corner.

Mrs. Leadbetter sat in the roadway and puffed. "MAD!" she shouted. A car came round the corner, the driver seeing Mrs. Leadbetter just in time. Braked tires squealed, and the car rocked as the driver swung the steering wheel. Mrs. Leadbetter rolled over and got onto her hands and knees. Mr. Macken, coming to see what the noise was about, found her thus, the broken branches around her.

"Don't move!" he shouted. "I'll be right there." He put his hands on her shoulders and turned her over. "Just take it quietly. Lie down for a bit."

"GET YOUR HANDS OFF OF ME!" Frustrated both at her attempt to help and her attempt to get up, Mrs. Leadbetter was getting redder and redder.

A sleepy Mr. Vichelli came out, his T-shirt still rumpled from where he'd been having a quiet nap. "Goddamighty, Mrs. Leadbetter, what were you doing up that tree?"

Mrs. Leadbetter began to cry. "IT'S THAT STUPID BOY!" she ranted. "I DON'T KNOW WHY . . . I WOULDN'T GIVE HIM TUCKER IF HE WAS MINE. HIM AND HIS STUPID CAT."

"Calm yourself, Mrs. Leadbetter. Please."

"WELL, WHAT WOULD YOU HAVE DONE? LEFT HIM UP THERE? SOMEONE HAD TO RESCUE THE POOR CREATURE!" Mrs. Leadbetter was still speaking fortissimo.

"You went up the tree after the cat?" Mr. Vichelli's voice was full of admiration. "He woulda come down in the dark, you know."

"SHUT UP!" Mrs. Leadbetter turned on Mr. Vichelli, who retreated, shrugging.

"She's all yours," he said, scratching his stomach and winking at Mr. Macken.

"Mrs. Leadbetter, whatever's the matter? Father, what's going on out here? Come on now, dear, up you get. I've just made a pot of tea. Come along." Mrs. Macken patted Mrs. Leadbetter's shoulder, stood back as that lady heaved herself upright, and led her inside. Mr. Macken began to gather up the broken branches. He looked up and noted that the cat was no longer in the tree.

"*Prr-wow?*" Seville sat on the parapet and cleaned his face. The man laughed. "Hi, cat!" He dumped the branches on the rubbish pile and went in search of his son.

Mrs. Leadbetter had calmed down with the tea and sympathy. "He was on the awning, coaxing that blessed cat. I near killed meself laughing. The cat would come a bit and then go back. I was having bets with Art about how long it'd be before he lost his cool. He did. I knew he would! That flaming hair's a sign of temper. Strange that none of the others has it, isn't it, Mrs. Macken? Still, you never can tell with things like that. And then he fell off, of course, and the cat jumped onto the roof easy as a butterfly."

"Why don't you like him?" Clare's voice was gruff.

"OH, YOU DID FRIGHTEN ME, CLARE. I DIDN'T SAY I DIDN'T LIKE HIM. . . ."

"Did you say Cass fell off the parapet? Where is he now?"

"I dunno, Mrs. Macken. He shouted 'HELP' and bolted."

Clare got up and left the room. "Dad! Dad!" she called. "Where's Cass?"

They found him on the stair going down into the shop. He had a packet of Band-Aids and was trying to patch a jagged tear on his leg. The blood ran thick and red and the Band-Aids would not stick on. He made no resistance when his father took the packet from him. "You'd better come on up and get that seen to," his father said quietly.

"Get *her* out of the way, please," Cass begged, gesturing upward. Mrs. Leadbetter's voice seemed to fill the house.

"Never mind her. Can you walk?"

"Course I can walk!" But Cass found his legs were wobbly. His father helped him up the stairs and into the bathroom, Clare hovering round them. "Get Mother, Clare."

Clare wasted no time. She did not wait for Mrs. Leadbetter to finish her dissertation on inherited traits, but tugged at her

mother's hand. "Excuse me a minute, please, Mrs. Leadbetter."
Mrs. Macken could see from Clare's face that something was
wrong. She followed her daughter to the bathroom. Mrs.
Leadbetter, determined not to be left out of anything, came
behind her.

"I wouldn't muck about with that, Mr. Macken. I'd take
him up to Outpatients. It'll need stitches, that, or I'm me un-
cle's father-in-law."

"I think that would be best, Father. You get the car out,
I'll clean him up a bit. Thanks, Mrs. Leadbetter. Mr. Macken
will let you out. Clare, get me a thick towel, pet, please."

"And all for a stubborn coot of a cat!" Cass said bitterly.

They put seven stitches in the wound and gave Cass an anti-
tetanus injection. He was left lying on the high bed to rest
for a while before they would let him go home. Behind the
screens in another part of the room he heard two people
talking. "But what I can't get over is why should anyone want
to break into a clothes closet?"

"Was Mr. Bywater upset about it?"

"No. Just smiled and said, 'Well they won't find anything,'
and asked for a drink of water."

"Sister was mad. . . ." There was laughter and then the
nurses, Cass supposed they were nurses, moved away.

A hot potato

CASS LAY AWAKE listening to the different traffic noises coming clearly from the harbor bridge and thought about Mr. Bywater. His leg ached. He had a cold feeling in his stomach. It couldn't have been a coincidence. Vichelli's broken into, an attempt made on Macken's, and Mr. Bywater's clothes closet at the hospital. It was all right for Mr. Bywater, oh, yes. "They won't find anything," he'd said. No, and why? Because he'd passed it on to me, Cass thought. Big deal!

What had seemed an ordinary request from a stricken man had suddenly gone sour. Should he tell his father? "Don't tell . . . ," the man had said. Don't tell who? Don't tell what? He argued with himself for some time. He'd accepted the trust so lightly. But the attempted break-in and the wrecking of the laundry might have been part of the Vichelli operation. Anyway, nobody could possibly know that Mr. Bywater had given him anything. Or could they? There was that black Mercedes with two men in the front. It had driven past while Cass was kneeling beside Mr. Bywater. There was the young man whose footsteps Cass had not heard approaching; he could have been watching.

Cass got out of bed, suppressing a groan. His leg had stiffened up. He found the key ring and sat on the side of the bed feeling its shape. He would have to find a good hiding place for it; he couldn't just keep carting it around with him —too risky. One day, he'd forget and leave it in his pocket and it would be discovered in the wash. There would be questions. No, he'd have to keep it until Mr. Bywater was well enough to take charge of it again. He could hide it in the storeroom.

It was a very vivid dream. Two gunmen in the shop, one pointing a gun at Alanna Caterina, one at Mrs. Macken, and a third man tearing the storeroom apart. Cass woke up sweating. He turned over, favoring his leg, and went straight back to sleep.

The hard knob of the button and keys in his pocket nagged at Cass all through the next day. He got a lot of teasing about his leg but turned it off by dramatizing his terror that Mrs. Leadbetter was going to give him artificial respiration. Everyone knew Mrs. Leadbetter and her zeal for using her St. John's. Cass was always sending her up. With that and the Vichelli break-in Cass had a busy day being the center of attention.

It was on his way home that afternoon that Cass first thought of the ideal place to hide the key ring. Father O'Donovan wouldn't mind. He turned aside and entered the cool stillness of the church. He had been in the presbytery often enough but never before in Father O'Donovan's church. He slid into a pew and waited until his heart stopped thudding so hard, gripping the key ring inside his pocket. The statues of the saints all seemed to be staring at him; even the fishermen mending their nets in the big stained-glass window appeared to stare past Jesus, who was calling them to be fishers of men, right into his soul.

Cass felt ashamed. He felt angry, too. The anger rose up inside him, choking him. It wasn't fair, giving him something that brought trouble, making him promise to keep it and not tell. At first, he did not see the movement near the altar, then he was aware of Father O'Donovan coming down the aisle toward him. The priest was no longer funny. In his black soutane he was different, though his eyes were still the same, full of understanding and wisdom and laughter. He slid into the pew in front of Cass and sat sideways facing him. "Have you got troubles, Cassowary?"

Cass nodded.

"Do you want to tell me?"

Again Cass nodded.

The silence stretched on and on. "I won't bite you. And I won't tell," the priest said at last.

Cass smiled. "Thank you, Father O'Donovan. I guess . . . I guess it's just something I have to wear by myself. But thanks, anyway. I was . . . I was going to do something really mean."

"And now you've changed your mind." It was a statement, not a question.

"Yes." Cass hesitated. "I was going to make a convenience of your church."

"God knows She's used to it," the old man murmured. He looked keenly at the boy, loving him. "You'll be late home and the shop getting busy. You go, and I'll say a prayer for you."

Cass nodded. He touched the old man's hand in a gesture of friendliness before he limped out. He was glad that he hadn't hidden the key ring under one of the saints. It didn't seem like a good idea any more; he couldn't understand now why it had seemed the ideal solution when he first thought of it. He began to hurry.

Alanna Caterina was on his back as soon as he hit the shop, scolding him for being late. "Get a move on, Cass. Shake that leg. Even seven stitches can't make you that slow."

"Leave him alone, Alanna Caterina. Cass, get yourself something to eat while you're changing. Are you O.K.?"

"Thanks, Mum. Yes, I'm fine. Keep your hair on, sister dear. Your temper is showing."

Alanna threw a packet of crumpets at him. Cass fielded them, tossed them into the air, crowing "Owzatt?" and then scored a direct hit on Alanna's back from the stairway.

Later, in the storeroom, Mrs. Macken stood watching Cass load the trolley to restock the shelves. "Leg hurting?" she asked.

"A bit. Nothing to worry about. It's a bit stiff, that's all. What's biting Alanna Caterina today?"

Mrs. Macken laughed. "Boy troubles, as usual. Vincent is so jealous of Trevor he tried to make Alanna promise she'd never see him again."

Cass whistled. "That was asking for it, wasn't it?"

"It certainly was. *And* he got it, too. You can imagine!" Cass nodded. "What made you late, son?"

"I was talking to Father O'Donovan. He's a beaut bloke, Mum, don't you reckon?"

"One of the best. As long as you're all right, Cass, that's the main thing."

"Don't worry, Mum. I'm O.K." He started pushing the trolley through to the shop. "Sorry I was late."

"Not to mention. Oh, by the way, there's a new price list, so you can have a sitting-down job doing the labels once you've done the fixtures."

"Righto, Mum."

Mrs. Macken sighed. Sometimes she wondered if their lives were too disciplined—if it was fair to take so much from the other members of the family so that Clare would not be too disadvantaged by her deafness. Clare had started special schooling when she was three, each word repeated hundreds and hundreds of times before she mastered it. She needed to practice her speaking all the time to gain tone control. Now she was a pupil at a private school and competing with children whose hearing was normal. It was constant work for Clare and for every member of the family, but no one grumbled. Alanna Caterina shrugged off thoughts of university and helped in the shop. Cass gave up his afternoons and Saturday mornings. Mr. Macken gave up his leisure hours. She . . . mothers were expected to make sacrifices for their children. She got so tired. The extra lessons to help Clare with vocabulary and speech, the care never to let her impatience and weariness show to the children took their toll. She leaned her head against a stack of cartons. She heard Clare come in, calling greetings to her sister and brother, and their joyful response. Mrs. Macken straightened up. Of course it was worth it! She went out into the shop, a smile on her face.

Father O'Donovan's church was vandalized that night. Books scattered, statues overturned, the money from the offertory box tipped out in a kind of contempt for the small coins, candles broken and ground into the floor. Cass tried to tell himself it was coincidence. Just because he had been in the church for half an hour didn't mean that it was because of him the church had been broken into. That was just too fantastic. He thought he had convinced himself, but a nasty nagging voice in the back of his mind kept saying, "It was, you know. It was because of you."

"I've got to find somewhere safe," he said to himself. "Somewhere handy, but safe. I wish he hadn't asked me to keep it for him." The solution flashed across his mind almost immediately. If Mr. Bywater's clothes closet had been broken into at the hospital, *they* wouldn't look there again. He would just take it up to the hospital and ask them to put the key ring with Mr. Bywater's things. He felt cheered immediately and went whistling lightheartedly around the shop.

He didn't know Father O'Donovan had come in until he

heard Mrs. Leadbetter's voice. "Do they know who done it, Father?"

"No, Mrs. Leadbetter. No, they don't."

"A terrible thing, Father! Did they pinch anything?"

"Not that I know of. Not even the money out of the box, unless there was more in it than usual."

"Then tell me, why would anyone do such a thing? They'd have to be sick, Father, to do a thing like that, now wouldn't you say so?"

"Excuse me, please," Cass said, steering his trolley past Mrs. Leadbetter.

"Ho, and how's the leg today? Been up any more trees?"

"O.K., thanks, Mrs. Leadbetter."

"Funniest thing I ever saw, Father. Cass up a tree trying to coax the cat to come down, and of course he fell!"

"Don't you know cassowaries can't fly?" The old man winked at Cass as he spoke.

"Could you spare a minute, Father?"

"For you I'd spare two. Lead on."

Cass pushed the empty trolley ahead of him into the storeroom and slid the door shut. He could hear Alanna Caterina engaging Mrs. Leadbetter in comment about the private life of a TV star. Good old Alanna! There were times when she was really spot on. "It was my fault." Cass faced the priest.

"Did you do it, Cassowary?"

"No!" Cass was horrified.

"Did you tell someone else to do it?"

"No. But, see, I think I've got something someone's after and they probably saw me go into the church yesterday. I was . . . I did think of hiding it under one of the statues." There, it was out.

Father O'Donovan sat on a bulk tin of lollipops. "Stop blaming yourself, Cassowary. It was just a coincidence."

"That's what I told myself at first, but . . . ."

"And that's all it is. This is life, me boy, not a TV script. Stop worrying about it."

"I still feel responsible. Deep down, I mean."

"That's just your guilty conscience about your intention. You're attaching too much importance to yourself. Stand back and have a good laugh at Cassowary Macken and you'll feel better." He got up and moved across to the door. "By the way, what do you do when someone chucks you a hot potato?"

Cass grinned. "Chuck it back!" he said promptly.

"Well . . . ?"

"Thanks, Father. Thanks a lot." He watched the priest trying to get out of the shop before Mrs. Leadbetter could see him but she chased after him. Cass went on with his work feeling lighthearted now. Father O'Donovan had confirmed his earlier thought. He knew what he must do. Mr. Bywater had to take his key ring back.

It wasn't as easy as that. When Mr. Macken took Cass to the hospital to have the stitches out, they were told yes, they could visit Mr. Bywater for a short time. He already had a visitor, and Cass did not get a chance to say anything. He got behind his father and the other man and took out the key ring and dangled it. Mr. Bywater made a funny sound, shook his head and went deathly white. Cass quickly put his hands in his pockets, and then a nurse rushed in and made them go out. "No use waiting, Stewart, come along." Mr. Macken nodded to the other visitor.

"Are there any messages you'd like me to give him?" the other man asked.

"No, thanks. We just wanted to know how he was getting along." The man turned away. Cass did not like him; he had a funny smell.

"I wonder what brought that on?" Mr. Macken said. "He's still a very sick man, I'd say. Well, at least he's got friends to visit him."

Cass did not answer. He was staring after a white-coated figure going down one of the corridors. It was the young man who had said he was not a doctor the morning Mr. Bywater had his attack; the one who had approached so quietly along the footpath that Cass had not heard him coming.

In the end, it was Seville who gave him the idea. He yowled outside the window until Cass got out of bed to let him in. The moonlight fell gently on the corrugated iron and threw the shadow of the parapet across it. Cass remembered the tennis ball. He had another one somewhere.

He found it and cut along the seam, making a hole big enough to take the key ring. He sealed it carefully with his superglue and then shaved some of the fur off one side of the ball. It would be funny if someone mistook him for a burglar, Cass thought, as he lowered himself onto the verandah roof. He glued the ball to the parapet just above the gutter so that it looked as if it was resting naturally, and went back to bed.

Gatecrasher at the sing-in

THERE WAS A LARGE GATHERING in the Macken home the next
Saturday evening—Alanna Caterina's boyfriends, the Vichellis, who had brought some relatives, Peter Graham, who
brought a wino who could do impersonations, Cass's mate
Rowdy Brisden was there sitting crosslegged in a corner and
saying nothing, as usual, and Mrs. Leadbetter had come on
the pretext of finding out how Cass's leg was healing. She sat
in a large armchair, her eyes darting from one to the other
of the people in the room, missing nothing, quite determined
to stay. Cass saw Clare get up and move across behind Father
O'Donovan. It made him angry and he could feel the color
coming up into his face.

"Cassowary!"

"Yes, Father?"

"It's getting dark, me boy. I have it on good authority. The
word is 'keep it pale.' "

Cass laughed. "O.K." No good trying to keep things from
Clare; she could see the change in his aura. He waggled his
fingers at her and she poked out her tongue at him.

It must have been an hour later that the young man walked
in. They had just finished a sad song Mr. Vichelli had taught
them, reveling in the long drawn out notes and Mrs. Vichelli's
violin cadenza. "Er, hi there." Everyone looked round,
startled. The young man laughed and gestured with his hands.

47

"It sounded so good from outside I just had to come up," he said. "I hope you don't mind."

Cass glanced at his father, who was frowning. Mrs. Macken smiled. "Oh, we met you on the footpath, didn't we, the day Mr. Bywater had his heart attack. You're just in time for supper."

Alanna Caterina got up and went across. "Do you know anyone?" she asked. "I'll introduce you. What did you say your name was?" Cass was not listening. He was looking at Seville, who had jumped off Clare's lap and was stretching himself out, front legs, back legs, and then preparing to wash an ear. The cat stopped suddenly, looked round, then walked across the room.

The boy held his breath. The hair on the back of his neck bristled and cold hammers xylophoned down his spine. He wasn't seeing things . . . or was he? Seville was looking up at Alanna, tail twitching. The cat was there. The guy Alanna was introducing was there. Seville hadn't walked round his leg, but *through it*! Cass wrenched his eyes away and glanced at Clare. She was seeing it too. She had that intent look on her face that she got when she was concentrating.

"Out, Seville. Go on, out!" Alanna Caterina touched the cat with the toe of her sandal and went on with the introductions. The young man stood silently beside her. Cass couldn't stand it any longer. He got awkwardly to his feet and bumped into the man's legs. At least that was his intention. He had to know if there were legs there. He fell sprawling, raising cries of alarm or laughter from the people in the room. But, next minute, Alanna was helping him up, the young man standing coolly watching. Cass muttered an apology and left the room.

He sat on the side of his bed so angry he could hardly see.

He didn't know why he was angry. Yes, he did, he hated being made to look a fool. He slammed the small drawer of his chest, annoyed at its untidiness, and was suddenly cold, alert and aware. Cass had his faults, but leaving drawers open was not one of them. Someone had been in his room! Cass opened the drawer and looked inside it. No, it had not been imagination. The lid of the box in which he kept his coin collection was not quite on. A quick check showed him that nothing had been taken. The boy went through his other drawers, pulling them out, slamming them shut, and once more anger surged through him. The hide! The filthy hide!

Who?

Cass got a grip on himself. Was the intruder still around? Cass got his nose to work but could not discern any strange scent. Quickly he checked the other rooms, but there was no sign of anyone. He slipped down the stairway to the shop, but the door was shut tight. He fingered the chain round his neck, thinking. He had opened the small drawer to get it out before tea, and he'd shut the drawer again before leaving his room. He'd swear to that. It might have been Alanna looking for some gear. Yes, that would be it. She was careless with drawers.

"Cass? Cass! Supper. Hurry, I'm fighting to save you a scone."

"Coming," he called and went racing up the stairs.

"What happened to you?" Rowdy asked.

Cass bit into a scone and answered through the crumbs. "Oh, just checking something." He reached for another. "Did I miss anything?"

Rowdy shook his head. "Only Moke the Soak doing an impersonation of you falling around, and the new feller singing like Alanna."

Cass grinned. "Moke's good, isn't he? He could make his fortune if he wanted to."

Rowdy nodded. "He won't stay off it. Mr. Graham thinks he will, but I bet he won't."

"What are you two talking about, anything interesting?"

"The fatal charm of the demon drink," Cass answered, staring the newcomer in the eye.

"You're a bit young to be hooked, surely?"

"A sip here and a sip there from babyhood, it all adds up, you know."

Rowdy was looking at Cass with bright eyes and waiting for the laughter he expected. None came. The man, who had simply said his name was O'Mara, was taking Cass seriously. Then, with a sudden movement, he whipped out the chain Cass wore round his neck and stared at the small horseshoe on the end of it.

"What is it?" he asked.

Rowdy laughed. "Don't you know a horseshoe when you see one?" He nudged Cass in the ribs. "Tell him, Cass."

"It's a shoe my great-grandfather's pony wore. It's very lucky."

"A horse should have a hoof so small!" Rowdy crowed. He seemed prouder of it than Cass himself.

O'Mara turned it over and over then shrugged and let it fall. "It would be more fun to wear the horse, surely?"

In spite of himself, Cass laughed. Alanna came up, eyebrows raised. "Can anyone else be in the joke?" she asked.

Rowdy went dumb, as he always did when girls were around. Cass said, "O'Mara suggested I should wear the horse and not the shoe." He dangled the horseshoe under his sister's eyes.

"You'll have to grow a bit," was all she said. She and O'Mara drifted away.

"What's his first name, Rowdy, did you catch it?"

"I dunno, Cass. I don't think he said. Just that his name was O'Mara."

"Perhaps his first name is O."

"D'you reckon?"

"Or Omar A," Cass muttered. He felt very tired, suddenly, as if his mind was being emptied out. For an instant he was back on the footpath with Mr. Bywater. Cass made a great effort and thought about golden syrup and Tickytacky Yumyum.

"WHAT ARE YOU TWO UP TO, EH?" Mrs. Leadbetter's voice boomed out.

"Nothin'," said Cass and Rowdy together.

"Tell that to the marines!" she said heartily. "Two boys get together, particularly you two, you can't help but be up to something. I'd say you're UP TO NO GOOD." Her voice rose again.

Peter Graham got up and went to sit beside Mrs. Leadbetter. Cass was grateful. The doorbell rang. "That'll be Dad," said Rowdy, glancing at his watch. "See you Monday, Cass. Thanks very much, Mrs. Macken. Bye all."

Mr. Macken went downstairs with Rowdy. When he came back, he went across to the group around Alanna. "Did you put the chain on the door when you came in, O'Mara?"

There was a small silence. "If it was on, I must have, mustn't I?" O'Mara had difficulty in controlling his contempt. Such a small thing to get inside a house, particularly a house with a cat door. Really, these humans were so dull! He was still annoyed at that clumsy boy falling into his figure image. He'd had to return to it before he was quite ready.

Mr. Macken nodded. Cass followed him out to the kitchen. "What's up, Dad?"

"I could swear I had the chain on the door after I let Mrs. Leadbetter in. She was last, wasn't she?"

"Yep. That's right. So how did O'Mara get in, is that it?"

"I must be getting forgetful in my old age, Stewart. Never mind."

"My window was open, Dad."

"D'you think he's got wings, son?"

"No, Dad, but what about if he climbed the tree and came across the roof?"

"An extraordinary way to gatecrash a party! Forget it, he seems a pleasant young man. I must have been careless and left the door on the latch, hoping Mrs. Leadbetter would be going again any minute."

"I bet she's got sore eyes!" Cass said angrily. "She's been so busy swiveling them round it's a wonder she can see at all!"

"Steady! She's interested, that's all."

"Telling me! I think I'll go to bed, Dad. Night."

Clare was fast asleep on the floor behind Father O'Donovan. Cass looked at her, hesitated, then decided not to say anything. Mrs. Leadbetter would only start shouting again. He said his good nights and went to his room. He had meant to ask O'Mara about being at the hospital. Too late. If he was a doctor he must be all right, though he'd said he wasn't when Mrs. Macken asked him. Everyone seemed to be getting on with him, anyway, particularly Alanna Caterina. Cass yawned. He shut his eyes and saw Mr. Bywater running down the footpath toward the shop. Cass blotted out the picture with another—himself wearing a horse on a chain round his neck. It made him sleepy.

Airy legs?

CASS FOUGHT HIS WAY BACK to consciousness, the weight of the horse smothering him. With a tremendous effort, he turned over and heard Clare giggle. She was sitting on his chest, waiting for him to wake up. "Oh, it's you! I thought it was a horse." He yawned. "Get off, you big lump, I can't breathe." He yawned again. "What's the time ever?"

"Six."

"It's Sunday!" Cass said indignantly. "Can't you let a feller get his beauty sleep?"

"No, Cass. Cass, listen. Last night . . . ."

"What about last night?" Cass sat up and clasped his hands round his knees. "I'm never bright in the mornings, you know that," he groaned.

"Seville . . . and that man. You saw, I know."

"Tell me first, what did you see?"

"Seville walked through his trouser leg."

Cass nodded. "I've been trying to kid myself it didn't happen. That's why I fell into him, through him . . . did you see what happened then?"

"You almost fell through him, but then he moved. He must have moved, because you fell flat."

"I sure did! I had to find out if he was real. What do you reckon?"

Clare picked up a pad and pencil and began to sketch, Cass watching. She often did this when words were hard for her.

One after the other, she drew the people who had been at the house the night before—the Vichellis and their relations, Father O'Donovan, Peter Graham, Moke the Soak, Alanna Caterina, Vincent looking daggers at Trevor, Rowdy, Mrs. Leadbetter, Cass, the Macken parents, and finally, O'Mara. Clare never drew people without their auras. Cass was interested to see that Mrs. Leadbetter was throwing out very long electric impulses and remembered Clare saying, "She sees so much." But O'Mara—Clare had drawn him the size of a Pygmy and filled in the outline with solid black. "Why?" Cass asked, pointing at it.

Clare shook her head. "It's how I saw him," she said. "Everything going in, not coming out, trying to get me in, too."

"You? I didn't see him speak to you."

"He doesn't. He gets inside my head. To make me tell him things."

"Oh, no! Oh, Clare, *no*! What sort of things?"

"About Mr. Bywater," Clare said flatly.

"But why? What do you know about Mr. Bywater?"

"Nothing, but he keeps putting Mr. Bywater in my head."

"I saw him up at the hospital," Cass said at last. "He was wearing a white coat. Do you think he's one of those psycho nuts? He told us he wasn't a doctor the morning Mr. Bywater passed out."

Clare did not answer. She was watching him closely. Cass said, "He put Mr. Bywater into my head too—well, I guess it was him, I had no other reason to think of him—but I thought of Tickytacky Yumyum instead."

Clare was delighted. "That gummed him up," she chortled. "And it was Alanna who helped you when you fell, not him. He didn't help all night, not passing round food, taking out cups, or anything."

"I didn't notice, I got mad."

"Yes, your aura went yukky green as you went out. I was chicken, Cass, I got behind Father O'Donovan and held on to his hand."

"Does O'Mara frighten you, Clare?"

Clare thought for a moment. "No. I got prickles up my back when Seville walked through him, but he doesn't frighten me the way Trevor does."

"*Trevor?*"

"The way he looks at me."

"I thought he never looked past his little sugarplum. If he looks at you again I'll smash his face in."

"Thanks, Cass. If he comes again, I'm going to pinch him."

"Who, Trevor?"

"No, O'Mara, to see if he's real."

"Everyone else thought he was O.K. It must be us who're queer." Cass was going to mention about the chain on the door, but didn't. No use scaring Clare. He didn't tell her about the open drawer, either. He wanted to talk to Alanna about that first. He was glad now that he hadn't told anyone about . . . he closed his mind. He would not think about the key ring.

Alanna said she hadn't been to his drawer. Mrs. Macken looked at Cass and said, "Why did you ask?"

"It was open," Cass said. "I never leave it open."

"There's always a first time, son, though I must say you are pretty good about things like that. It's not like you to get upset about an open drawer, though."

"I'm not upset, Mum, just that I like to know if someone's been at my things."

"Will you lend me your horseshoe chain, Cass?"

"Why?"

"I'm going out, and it is rather cute. Go on, say yes."

"Who're you going with?"

"Adam Spinks. He's new. He's been coming into the shop every day. He's got a Mercedes. Wowee! A black one!"

Cass whistled. "Take a good look at his teeth, Alanna. Remember Little Red Riding Hood."

"O.K., Grandma. Well, can I?"

"I s'pose. Look after it, though."

"Sure. Thanks, brother. Well, I'd better go and get ready." When she came back, Mr. Macken lifted his head out of the Sunday paper to look at her. She had on a black T-shirt, the horseshoe swinging down the front of it, and faded, tight blue jeans.

"Tell me," he said, "what would you wear for a Rolls Royce?"

"My white T-shirt, of course!" Alanna Caterina sounded surprised. Mr. Macken shook his head and returned to the paper.

Later, as the rest of the family walked up to church, the black Mercedes drove past them. The driver was different, but Cass was almost sure it was the car that had gone by the morning Mr. Bywater had his attack. Cass felt uneasy; he didn't like it. The old questions returned to haunt him: What had Mr. Bywater been up to? Why was he running? How did the key ring come into it? Who were *they*? "What's he like, Mum, this new feller of Alanna's?"

"Seems very nice. Well spoken, neatly dressed and adores Alanna. Why, Cass?"

"How old is he?"

"Oh, mid-twenties."

"Young to be driving a Mercedes."

"Stewart, you know I'm the father of this family?" Mr. Macken spoke sternly.

Cass laughed. "Of course, Dad!"

"Then just leave Alanna's boyfriends to me, eh? I've got my eagle eye on them, don't worry."

"O.K., Dad, you're welcome. Ask can you borrow the car. That will test his devotion!"

Alanna laughed off all inquiries when she got home. They had enjoyed the day, she said, and that was that.

"Are you seeing him again?"

"What's that to you, cheeky?"

"I want to know, that's all. No harm in asking."

"No guarantee that you'll get answered, either. But as a matter of fact, I am. On Wednesday."

"I guess if you go out with Vincent on Monday and Trevor on Tuesday and this guy Adam on Wednesday . . . ."

". . . and O'Mara on Thursday, what am I going to do about Friday and Sunday, eh? Is that it?"

"Are you going out with O'Mara, too?" Cass was goggle eyed.

"Why not? He's rather sweet. He's different."

"How 'different'?"

"You're asking far too many questions, my child."

"Well, how? I'm only asking. Don't you want me to be interested in what you do?"

"I'm not sure," Alanna said slowly, and would say no more. Cass didn't know which part of his question she was answering.

"What have you got against O'Mara, Cass?" his mother asked later.

"I haven't got anything against him, Mum. He is . . . well, different, isn't he?"

"Interesting rather than different. You sister can look after herself anyway. She earns her fun."

Mayday! Mayday!

"COME TO THE POOL WITH US, Cass?"

Cass grinned at Frosty and shook his head. "Can't."

"Aw, go on. It wouldn't hurt for once. Why can't you?"

"Got to help in the shop. You know that."

"Don't you ever get any time off?"

Cass ignored that question. "Have fun," he said. "See you tomorrow." He turned down the hill toward home, hearing the talk and laughter behind him and feeling resentful that he couldn't go with the gang. He sat on the thought so that it would not grow to be self-pity.

Alanna Caterina was not at her desk; there were no customers and no sign of Mrs. Macken. "Shop!" called Cass, giving the bell a ding as he went past.

"Coming!" Alanna Caterina emerged from the storeroom, laughing. "Oh, it's only you."

Cass staggered back, hand to heart. "Only me? *Only?* Ah, my little sugarplum, you slay me! Do I mean so little to you?"

"You wretch, you've been listening through keyholes," his sister said. "You don't deserve it, but I've a surprise for you."

Cass stood to attention. "Go on, then, surprise me."

"You won't need to do the shelves this afternoon. They're all done."

Cass looked round the shop. "So they are," he said. "That was kind of you. Had a slack day?"

"Oh, it wasn't my doing; it was O'Mara."

"You're quite right, you *do* surprise me!" Cass pushed open the storeroom door. "Thank you very much, O'Mara," he called.

O'Mara came from behind the far shelves. "Hi, Cass."

Cass withdrew. Why? Earlier he had felt resentment about his shop duties; now he felt resentment because they were done for him. The fellow was worming his way into the shop, even! What was he after? He remembered Clare pointing out that on Saturday night O'Mara had not helped anyone but himself. And how come he wasn't up at the hospital? He supposed they got time off like other people.

Mrs. Macken was upstairs. "May I go to the pool, Mum? O'Mara's done the shelves. Frosty and Rowdy and some of the kids are going. Say yes, go on, Mum, please?"

"Yes," said his mother obediently. "Show me that leg first." She gave it a close scrutiny then said, "O.K."

"Ripper!" Cass crowed and whirled his mother round three times and went off to change.

His mates were glad to see him and Cass enjoyed himself, forgetting about the shop completely. It must have been about quarter to five he heard Clare calling him. He knew, as clearly as if she were standing on the side of the pool, that she needed him. He swam quickly to the end and yelled a good-bye to the others.

Mrs. Leadbetter was coming out of the shop as Cass approached, but turned to say something to someone inside, so he ducked in through the yard and dropped his wet trunks and towel in the laundry. "If that old hippopotamus has been worrying Clare again I'll . . . I'll put treacle in her shoes!" he muttered.

It wasn't Mrs. Leadbetter. O'Mara stood behind Clare at

the transducer. He was making her repeat a series of words over and over again. Clare's face was pale. "By land," she said. "By air. By sea. By car. By train. By ferry. By water . . . ."

"Again," said O'Mara crisply. "That last one again. Bywater, Bywater, Bywater."

"I'm tired," Clare protested.

"LEAVE HER ALONE!" Cass launched himself at O'Mara.

Clare sobbed, "Oh, Mack, you came!" Cass hit the end of the table and howled with pain. There was nobody in the room but himself and Clare.

"Where did he go?" Cass panted.

"What's going on? Why are you shouting? Stewart, get hold of yourself!" Mr. Macken stood in the doorway.

"O'Mara was teasing Clare," Cass snarled, rubbing his sore ribs.

"Don't be ridiculous! O'Mara's been down in the shop doing your job all afternoon."

"Are you sure?"

"Of course I'm sure. He hasn't been out of my sight for the last hour."

"I swear he was standing behind her when I came up from the laundry and making her say . . . ."

"Shut up, Cass! It's all right, Dad. Sorry we made so much noise."

"You look tired, Clare. Perhaps you've done enough for today. O.K.? Stewart, you might like to come down and help clean up."

"O.K., Dad, I'll be right there."

"Now!" Mr. Macken didn't often raise his voice.

"Yes, sir!" Cass gave his sister a quick look as he left the room. She nodded her head at him and mouthed "Later."

"Enjoy yourself?"

"Yes, thanks, O'Mara." Cass was short. "I'll take over now."

He got the broom from the storeroom and began to clean up. Sweeping hurt his side and he wondered if he'd broken a rib.

"You're not very cheerful," Alanna Caterina said. "I would have thought you'd have been on top of the world having an afternoon off."

"Sure, an' I was born to be a drudge and not a playboy," mocked Cass, recovering. "Did you miss me?" He stopped near the check-out, leaning on his broom and making sheep's eyes at his sister.

Alanna dropped a bundle of notes she was counting, and Cass stooped to pick them up. Their heads were very close together. "To be honest, I did. There were times when O'Mara didn't seem to be . . . well, it was almost as if he weren't there. Still, I guess he's new to it. At least you don't stand round looking into space . . . and I'll have that one you put in your pocket, thank you," she added, straightening up.

"I didn't think you'd miss it," Cass giggled, handing it over. "Have you gone off him a bit, then?"

"No way! He fascinates me. Oh, Cass, there's some sugar spilled round near the soups. There wasn't time to clear it up when it happened. O.K.?"

"O.K.," replied Cass mechanically. He went on with his work, his mind busy. He'd have to talk to Clare. She *had* called him. They had always had this mental response to each other's needs.

O'Mara stayed on, so Cass and Clare had to wait for their talk. Alanna was very gay and there was a lot of laughter. Cass watched his parents; they seemed quite relaxed with their guest. He took no notice of Clare, and she sat in silence. O'Mara laughed when the others did, but there was something about the way he laughed. After a while, Cass pinned it down —his eyes did not change when he laughed.

"Do you work at the hospital, O'Mara?"

"No, Cass. What gave you that idea?"

"I saw you up there the other day. You had a white coat on. I reckoned you were a psycho nut."

"Cass!"

"It's O.K., Mum. What's wrong with that?" Cass waved his hands around. "Well, are you?"

"Guess again." Human children were even worse than adults, O'Mara thought.

"What do you do, O'Mara? If you don't mind me asking." Mr. Macken raised his eyebrows in a query.

"Travel. Search. Observe. It's an interesting occupation."

"Then what were you doing at the hospital?" Cass couldn't help asking.

O'Mara looked at him for a long time before he spoke. "How *is* Mr. Bywater?" he asked.

Clare got up abruptly and began to clear the table. Mrs. Macken nodded at Cass. "Give her a hand, son."

"O.K., Mum." As he went out to the kitchen with a pile of plates, Cass could hear his father answering O'Mara's question. Shortly afterward, Alanna and O'Mara went out.

"You did call me, didn't you, Clare?" Clare nodded. "Why?"

"I was working with Mum, and O'Mara came up and said he'd stay if she had anything to do. She wanted to get her hair cut. Alanna came and said O'Mara was needed in the shop again, and I just went on using the juicer. But O'Mara came back and made me say Bywater over and over and over. He was getting right into my mind, Cass. I couldn't hold on, so I called you."

"I'd like to know what he's getting at," Cass said. "Just as well I heard you when you called."

"You always do," Clare smiled.

"I swear he was standing behind you when I came in, and you were saying you were tired. I just saw red and went for him and hit the table. He was there, Clare, wasn't he?"

"I thought so, Cass."

"It's spooky. Mum and Dad don't seem to notice anything, and Alanna just thinks he's 'different'. Do you think we should say something?"

"What could we tell them? Dad said he'd been down in the shop when we thought he was up here. He's put us under a spell."

"Do you think that's what he does?"

"I don't know. I get ideas from his mind to mine. Like talking without words. I think he wants to do it that way. I don't like it, so I don't let myself listen."

"You're weird!"

"Weird yourself! It's no worse than your nose. How does he smell, Cass?"

"I don't know." Clare stared at him. Cass tried to think. "Mostly clothes," he said at last. "That's funny, too, come to think of it. I must have a good sniff at him next time."

Clare giggled. "I forgot to pinch him, Cass."

"Get Seville to scratch him, that should show him up!"

Ghosts, is it?

ALANNA WAS HAPPY. She loved to be popular, and the excitement of having O'Mara and Adam Spinks competing for her favors against Vincent and Trevor made her excited and more beautiful than ever. Cass grudgingly admitted that Spinks seemed a nice guy, he smelled all right. The only thing against him was that he hedged when asked about the Mercedes. No, it wasn't his father's; it wasn't his, either. Well, whose then? He swore Cass to secrecy and admitted it was hired. "There's a company that leases out these black Mercs. Real prestige jobs. Impresses the clients—or the birds! You won't tell your sister, will you?" Cass was disappointed. If Adam could hire one, so could anyone.

"At least," Cass said to himself, "I needn't go trying to connect him with anything sinister." He felt happier and began to relax. That was until he suspected that someone had been searching his room again. "Clare, have you been in my room?"

Clare shook her head. "Have *you* been in *mine?*"

The nerves in Cass's stomach jerked. "Why? Is anything wrong?"

"I think someone has been through my books."

Cass began to get hot. "Has that O'Mara been here again?" he demanded of Alanna.

"No, not this week. Only Adam. He had a day off, so he

64

came to lunch." Alanna laughed. "Actually, he was rather a lamb. He came up and got it for us, didn't he, Mum?"

"Yes. It was a nice change," Mrs. Macken admitted. "Why did you think O'Mara had been here, Cass?"

"Oh, nothing," Cass hedged. "I just thought he might have been."

Two days later, Cass was sitting on the side of his bed, thinking. He was staring into the mirror without seeing anything until a movement caught his eye. It was Adam coming out of the Macken parents' room and carefully closing the door. Cass sat perfectly still, holding his breath.

"CA-ASS?" It was Alanna, calling to him from the shop. The boy finished tying the laces on his sneakers and went slowly downstairs to his job. Adam was facing the stairs, leaning on the check-out and talking to Alanna. Just for a moment his face registered surprise as Cass came into the shop. Then, "Hi, Cass," he said, and turned back to Alanna.

"Cass, see if you can find a blackcurrant jelly, will you? I want one for an order. And hurry, please."

"O.K." The boy disappeared behind the rows of shelves. What could he say? The shop was getting busy. Every jelly he turned up was lemon or pineapple. He began stacking them methodically into piles so that he wouldn't have to sort through them twice.

What had Adam been up to? He might have been sent up to get something. No, the way he had shut the door and moved so quietly meant that he was there without anyone's knowledge. Just my luck, Cass thought. I'm jumpy, that's all. Suspicious. He began to think about Mr. Bywater and just then found the blackcurrant jelly. When he brought it round to Alanna, O'Mara was in the shop, but Adam had gone.

O'Mara looked intently at Cass, nodded, then turned away. Cass thought of golden syrup, molasses, runny honey. Runny. Running. Mr. Bywater. Cass jerked his thoughts away.

Seville came from behind a pile of cartons and rubbed against Cass's legs. Cass fondled his ears and ran his finger along the jaw line. Seville turned up his head and purred his pleasure. "Get Seville to scratch him." Cass remembered his conversation with Clare. He draped the cat round his shoulders and pulled a trolley loaded with bales of sugar out into the shop. A quick glance showed him that O'Mara was still there. Seville lay around his neck, an orange-barred collar, while Cass stacked the sugar. On the way back to the storeroom with the empty trolley, he stopped, plucked Seville from his neck and flung him at O'Mara. The cat screeched his displeasure, did a magnificent half-turn in midair and clawed at a shelf of washing powder. O'Mara turned to see what the noise was. He put out a hand, and Seville retreated, back arched, ears flattened, eyes blazing.

"Cass! Come and get your cat out of here!" Alanna was nearly as furious as Seville.

"Coming." Cass came out of the storeroom. "What's upset him?" he asked innocently. "What did you do to him, O'Mara?"

"Extended the hand of friendship," O'Mara drawled, keeping cool with great effort. He distrusted cats.

"He doesn't seem to like you much," Cass continued. "Perhaps it's your smell." He went close to the man and sniffed loudly. O'Mara retreated, looking alarmed. He would have to find his ank soon. He couldn't stand much more.

"Get that animal and yourself out of here!" hissed Alanna. "Scat!"

"I'm going," said Cass, aggrieved. "Come on, Seville, old

marmalade, we know where we're not welcome." He scooped up the cat and marched back to the storeroom.

"One thing I found out," Cass told Clare later, "Seville doesn't like him, and O'Mara got really edgy when I sniffed at him."

"Could you smell anything?"

"Cloth."

"Oh, that's odd, isn't it?"

"Yeah. You know, we're dumb clucks. All we have to do is ask Alanna. . . ."

"Ask Alanna what?" Their elder sister had come into the room as he spoke.

"What's it like when O'Mara kisses you?"

Alanna's hand came up with a jerk and caught Cass across the mouth. "Shut up!" she screamed. "Shut up shut up shut up!"

"Stop it, Alanna. Stewart, go to your room at once. Don't look so frightened, Clare. Now then, what's going on?" Mr. Macken put one arm round Clare and reached the other one toward Alanna Caterina.

"Oh, put yourself in a twin tub!" Alanna rushed out and slammed the door.

"What was all that about?"

"Nothing, Mum. Cass asked Alanna something and she went mad. She looks good when she gets mad, doesn't she?"

"Really, Clare!" Both parents were laughing. "You are a funny little thing."

"Can I come out?" Cass called through the door. "My lip's bleeding and I need to drip in the bathroom, not on the carpet."

"Don't you dare drop blood on the carpet. Hurry up. Here, let me look." Mrs. Macken hurried out.

"Mum?"

"Huh?" Mrs. Macken finished dabbing. She met her son's eyes in the bathroom mirror.

"Mum, did you or Dad send Adam up to your room to get anything today?"

"Certainly not. What put that idea into your head?"

"I saw him coming out very quietly and shutting the door. Just after I got home from school. I was sitting on the side of my bed and looking in the mirror—well, not looking, just staring at nothing, you know how you do sometimes, and there he was. And Clare says someone's been at her books, and I'm nearly sure someone's been through my things. . . ."

"What a horrible thing you are saying, Cass! He's a nice guy and Alanna's very fond of him. I'm sure you're mistaken."

"I quite like him myself, Mum, but . . . well, it's a bit rough, isn't it, him going into your room like that?"

"Did you speak to him?"

"No, Mum."

"Then don't. I'll talk to your father, and he will deal with it."

"O.K., Mum. Mum, can I go out for a bit? I want to have a yarn with Father O'Donovan."

"All right. Don't be late."

"Thanks, Mum. See you later." Cass slipped out down the back stairs and ran along the street. Five minutes later, he was knocking at the presbytery door.

"Who is it?"

" 'It's me, Piglet,' " answered Cass.

"Come round to the side window, then, Cassowary. Can you get in over the sill?" The old man was sitting in a chair with his bare feet in a dish of water. "Excuse me not getting up. Would you care to join me? There's plenty of room."

"No, thanks, Father. Are they sore, your feet?"

"Like the Little Mermaid's, me boy. It's only God's love keeps me going. Perhaps you'd like to put your face in the dish, eh? Run into something, did you?"

"Alanna cracked me one," Cass laughed, fingering his puffy lip.

"Is that why you came?"

"No." Cass drew a deep breath. "Can I ask you something?"

"Anything at all."

"Well, it's this. Father O'Donovan, do you believe in ghosts?"

"I don't disbelieve in 'em," said the old man, slowly. "What sort of a ghost would you be thinking of? Headless horrors walking midnight corridors with clanking chains and horrid groans? Wispy ladies clothed in gallons of tears and wringing bloodstained hands? Eh? That sort, do you mean?"

"No, not that sort, Father. Things that look solid but that a cat walks through. Things that you'd swear are there but aren't when you go to touch them."

"Nip into the kitchen and put on the kettle, there's a good lad. If we're going to talk about ghosts we'll need something to keep out the cold. You'll find the tea in the cannister marked *Lent* and sugar in the canister marked *Borrowed*. There's no milk; can you drink it black? And I'll have the rest of the kettle in the basin here, thank you, Cassowary."

"O.K., Father. Where do you empty your tea leaves?" Cass made the tea and brought in the pot and two mugs. "Kettle coming up," he said and went back for it.

"There might be some biscuits left in that tin marked *Bait*, Cassowary. Mrs. Leadbetter made them, so they're tainted."

"They look all right to me," Cass called.

"Taint enough of 'em, Cassowary. Caught you that time! Now then, ghosts, is it? Did I ever tell you about the time that . . . ?"

An hour later, Cass scurried home, his spine still tingling from Father O'Donovan's stories of ghosts he had known or heard about back in Ireland. His mother let him in, exclaiming at his white face. "We've been talking about ghosts," Cass explained.

"I'll have a piece of him next time I see him, frightening you with ghost stories at this time of night. Hop into the shower, son, and get off to bed. Good night."

"Good night, Mum, Dad. I wasn't really frightened. . . ."

"Not much!" muttered Mr. Macken. "By the way," he asked his wife, "What did he do to make Alanna Caterina so mad?"

"Asked her what it was like when O'Mara kissed her."

"Cheeky young devil!"

"Yes, but the point is that O'Mara never has. Never even tried to."

"Oh, dear. Yes, well that would make any beautiful girl mad, wouldn't it? I wonder . . . . Oh, well."

Under the shower, Cass suddenly realized that Father O'Donovan hadn't talked about the sort of ghosts who seemed to be there but weren't.

Invitation to a party

"THERE'S A PARTY. At Elfina's place at Castle Hill. All the class is going. Mum, can I go? Please say yes, Mum." Mrs. Macken looked at Clare's eager face.

"When is it, Clare?"

"Next Wednesday after school. We're going in a bus, and there's a pool and a barbecue and everything! Say yes! I'll die if you don't."

"I'll talk to your father, that's as much as I can promise at the moment." Clare hugged her mother.

"Thanks, Mum. Dad will say yes if you ask him." Mrs. Macken smiled to herself. The private school for girls which Clare attended had made a big difference to the child. It was worth every bit of the extra money it cost.

Elfina Davenport had begun to make a fuss of Clare after Clare's essay on Mr. Bywater's heart attack had been read to the class. She had told her father, she said, and he thought it was marvelous of the Mackens to look after the unfortunate man.

Clare looked as if she was lit up from inside. "I'll tell Cass," she said. Mrs. Macken could hear her out in the storeroom talking excitedly.

Cass stopped stamping prices on cake mix packets. "Sounds ripper, Clare. Did Mum say you could go?" A shadow clouded the brightness of Clare's face. Then she cheered up again.

"She'd ask Dad, and Dad's sure to say yes." Cass went on with his stamping. "Won't he, Cass? Won't he say yes?"

"If you asked him and looked at him like that, he'd say yes to anything," Cass laughed. "You really want to go, don't you?"

"Oh, *yes!*" Clare climbed up onto the bulk stock shelves and straddled the passageway. "I'm a bridge! I'm a tower! I'm a . . . !" She fell off in a heap as Cass tickled her leg. "You're mean. I'm going. Good-bye."

"See you later." Cass went back to work, laughing.

"YOU'RE LOOKING VERY PLEASED WITH YOURSELF, CLARE." Mrs. Leadbetter barred the way to the stairs.

Clare stopped. Even Mrs. Leadbetter looked lovely in the glow of the hope of a party. "Yes," she smiled. "And how are YOU, Mrs. Leadbetter?" She stood on tiptoe as she spoke the "you" and shouted it in Mrs. Leadbetter's ear.

Mrs. Leadbetter sprang back. "I'M NOT DEAF!" she roared. "THERE'S NO NEED TO SHOUT AT ME!" She regarded Clare's innocent face with suspicion. Had she done it on purpose? "SO WHAT'S NEW WITH YOU? SANTA CLAUS COMING EARLY?"

"I'm going to a party," said Clare, adding under her breath, "I hope."

"Where?" Mrs. Leadbetter lowered her voice.

"At Elfina Davenport's at Castle Hill. All the class is going in a bus." There. She'd committed herself now. Dad would have to let her go. Her old unease at being alone with Mrs. Leadbetter returned in a rush. "Excuse me, please," she said. She progressed up the stairs in a series of jumps, punctuating each leap with "Hoo!" or "Ha!"

Next day there was a letter to the parents giving details of the party and arrangements for transport. Mr. Macken said yes, Clare might go. Clare hugged him, then rushed to her mother and began to kiss her, saying "I see you." Kiss. "I see

you again." Kiss kiss. "I see you again." Kiss kiss. "I see you
again. . . ."

"For goodness' sake, Clare!" Mrs. Macken was weak from
laughter. It had been suggested to the children at Sunday
School one Mother's Day that they should kiss their mothers
every time they saw them. It was a sure way to make Mrs.
Macken giggle until she was helpless.

Mrs. Leadbetter came over to the shop to buy herself a
cool drink. "I'll drink it here, 'lanna," she said, wedging her
bulk against the check-out so that she could watch everyone.
Cass retreated to the stairs with his label marker. He had
taken to spending more time in the store itself so that he
could watch Adam and O'Mara if they came in. O'Mara arrived shortly afterward, greeted Alanna and Mrs. Leadbetter, then wandered across to Cass.

"Keeping you busy?" he asked, but he was watching Mrs.
Leadbetter. Cass nodded.

"How's that feller getting on, you know the one that collapsed outside the shop? Do you ever go to see him?" Mrs.
Leadbetter asked suddenly.

"I like my men healthy, thank you." Alanna was laughing.

"You and your men! Well, does your father go to see him?"

"He and Cass have been up a couple of times." Alanna rang
up and packed a small order. "Thank you, Mrs. Meakin. Can
you manage, or would you like Cass to help you home with
them?"

Mrs. Meakin shook her head. "I can manage, thanks."

"She's a fool," said Mrs. Leadbetter almost before the
woman was out of earshot. " 'Always take advantage of help,'
my mother told me, and it's a thing I've always done. You
never know when you'll need your strength. That feller now,
he didn't have enough or he wouldn'ta fell over like that. I
do wish your dad had called me!" She took a large gulp of

her drink and returned to the attack. "I wonder did he . . . I wonder will you get anything out of it?"

Alanna counted notes and slipped rubber bands round the bundles. O'Mara leaned against a shelf watching Mrs. Leadbetter. Cass watched O'Mara. Was he getting into Mrs. Leadbetter's mind? That "I wonder did" changed to "I wonder will." Was it a slip?

"After all," Mrs. Leadbetter threw her empty can into the bin, "he'da died if your dad hadn'ta helped him."

"He might send us a lottery ticket if we're lucky," Alanna Caterina said briskly. She nodded to Adam, who had just walked in. He went across to talk to Mr. Macken.

"He ought've give you something. HELLO, CLARE, WHEN'S THE PARTY?" Clare had come in through the side door.

"Wednesday, Mrs. Leadbetter. Alanna, can I get some ribbon from your room?"

"THEM DAVENPORTS GOT A BIG PLACE, HAVE THEY? AT CASTLE HILL, ISN'T IT?"

Clare nodded. "Can I, Alanna?"

"I'll come up as soon as we're closed and get it for you. O.K.?"

"O.K." Clare turned toward the stairs, saw O'Mara, and hesitated.

Cass, watching O'Mara and Adam, was aware that they were both looking at Clare. He stood up suddenly and said loudly, "There's a funny smell in here. Can you notice it, Alanna?" He walked toward the check-out, nose twitching, sniffed at Mrs. Leadbetter, who hit him on the head with her change purse, and walked on toward Adam.

"It's not me, Cass! I use all the right products. Got to keep sweet with your sister!"

Cass walked on. "It's something. Can't you smell it?" He sniffed loudly. "Very offensive, it is. Ah!" He had come round the other lane and was right behind O'Mara. He sniffed again. O'Mara sprang away and walked rapidly out of the shop. He couldn't afford to get angry. It used too much of his fast diminishing power.

Alanna was furious. Before she could speak, her father moved. "I'll deal with this," he said. "Stewart, go to your room and wait till I come." Cass went.

"Are you certain he isn't a changeling, Mr. Macken? He's not a bit like the others. You poor souls . . . ."

"AND YOU'RE A BIG FAT BAG OF WIND!" Cass shouted down the stairs, his temper getting the better of his caution. "WHY DON'T YOU MIND YOUR OWN BUSINESS?"

Down in the shop Mrs. Leadbetter laughed. "He's got spirit, I'll say that for him," she chuckled. "Don't be too hard on him, Mr. Macken, I guess I've been riding him a bit lately." She picked up her purse and went out, stopping to talk to O'Mara, who was standing in front of Vichelli's.

Later, upstairs, Mr. Macken looked at his son. "You're getting too big to belt, Stewart. . . ."

"No I'm not, Dad. I'd rather have a belting than a lecture. Honest. I reckon I deserve it." He bent over.

"Stand up!" his father said roughly. He held out his hand. "Shake, son. I've been wanting to say that to her for years!"

Cass chortled gleefully, grasping his father's hand in a strong grip.

"But . . . ." and Mr. Macken spent five minutes lecturing Cass on acceptable behavior, particularly when it concerned the keeping of goodwill and the earning of the family living. The boy wriggled and said "Yes, Dad" every now and then. You could never tell with parents. He hated being talked at.

It was the next day that Seville went missing. Cass looked for him in his usual haunts and did not find him. He wasn't worried. The cat sometimes didn't come home for a day, and as Alanna said, he was so well fed he wouldn't miss his tucker for a week.

On the third day, Cass began a systematic search of the district, looking gloomily for a squashed body. "I can't believe he's got so old and slow he'd let a car get him," he told Clare, "but I'd better make sure." He began with Harbor Street from Florence Avenue and then followed Wharf Road down to Peterlee Drive, which ran round the foreshore. The harbor flotsam bobbed against the stone wall near the ferry wharf, but there were no cats in the water that he could see. Perhaps O'Mara had done away with him. Cass considered this coldly. It seemed unreasonable. He shrugged and walked on, glancing across the water at the jagged city skyline and the yawning Opera House, up Iona Avenue, digressing into Mitiamo Close and Gabriel Court and back to Harbor Street. He heard a cat in Kettle Lane and ran, but it was not Seville. Zig Zag Street was a blank, and he followed it back to Florence Avenue.

Zig Zag Street was on a cliff which dropped abruptly to the flatness of Harbor Street, its slopes a mass of lantana, blackberries and small trees. Built in the apex of one of the street's angles was an old stone house, its grounds a tangle of unchecked shrubs and trees. A flight of stone steps went down from the street to it, only used now by water from a leaky pipe that fed a slippery weed growth. Below the house, the steps continued for a while but crumbled to nothingness in the jungle of lantana down the cliff face. It had belonged to an old lady who had died before Cass was born, her will so complicated that the property remained unsold and unoccupied.

Thinking about the house, Cass went back to it. Knowing how cats hated water between the toes, he didn't think Seville would have gone down the steps, but he'd better make sure. He called and called as he searched, but the only sign of life was a large rat, which scurried away as the boy approached. He'd already searched the bottom of the cliff.

"Any sign of him?" Mrs. Macken asked when Cass returned.

"Nope." Cass shook his head. "Not even in the gutter," he added bitterly.

"I wondered about that, too. It's the longest he's ever been away, isn't it?"

"Yes, Mum. I hope he's enjoying himself, wherever he is."

"He'll turn up." Alanna spoke confidently. "He's too old and ugly not to."

Cass sniffed. "I wouldn't be surprised if that O'Mara had done away with him."

"I don't know what's the matter with you," Alanna stormed. "You blame O'Mara for everything, and the way you go round sniffing at him is enough to make anyone want to get back at you!"

"Then he *has* done away with Seville?" Cass tried to keep his voice calm.

"No. Of course not. I don't know. Why don't you ask him?" His sister walked out.

"I might just do that," Cass shouted after her.

"Calm down, son. Just take it gently. Alanna's having a hard time just now."

"Big deal!" Cass sniffed. "She's the only one, I suppose?"

"Have you asked Mrs. Leadbetter?" Clare broke the silence.

"That old . . . ?" Cass began.

"Cass! That's enough."

". . . fairy godmother, I was going to say," finished Cass. "Do you think she'd know, Clare? Honestly, I mean?"

"She just might," Clare said slowly. "It's hard to know with her. Those fat eyes see everything that goes on. They're like a . . . like a vacuum cleaner sucking away."

Cass went across to see her, but Mrs. Leadbetter shook her head. "No, I haven't seen your cat. Fond of him, eh? Doesn't do to give your heart to an animal. I often says that to Art with his birds. They tear it to bits in the end, I told him, and they will. You'd best keep an eye open for a kitten. It's the only way to heal a loss. Get a new one and forget the old. Life must go on."

Cass tried to keep his indignation in check. "Yes. Thanks, Mrs. Leadbetter," he said. "I guess that's a great comfort to your husband."

Mrs. Leadbetter looked at Cass and went suddenly white. "You'd not compare an animal with a *human?*" She sounded shocked.

"Seville is human to me," said Cass. "Good-bye, Mrs. Leadbetter. If you do see him, you will let me know, won't you?"

"Yes," Mrs. Leadbetter said absently.

Father O'Donovan was sympathetic but agreed in principle with Mrs. Leadbetter. "If it had been a dog, now," he said. "But a cat . . . cats belong to themselves. They never give you the loyalty a dog does. Don't give up, Cassowary. He'll come home yet, you'll see."

Cass wanted to ask if he'd pray for Seville but couldn't quite bring himself to the point. Peter Graham offered to and Cass accepted eagerly. Peter shut his eyes and said, "We thank You and praise You, Lord, that Cass Macken's cat Seville is missing. He means a lot to Cass. We know that You are all-loving and want what is best for us. We are in Your hands, trusting You to do what is for our good. Give Cass peace of mind and a perfect faith. . . ."

"I ca-an't!" Cass burst out. "I can't thank God that Seville is missing!" He looked wildly at the young man in front of him. "It wouldn't be . . . it wouldn't be natural!"

"True. But it's scriptural. We are told to give thanks in *everything*. Praise and thanksgiving are the rockets that bear our prayers to God. Would you trust Seville to God?"

Cass hesitated for a long time. "I suppose so," he said grudgingly. "I guess I'll have to."

"Then just tell Him, eh?"

Cass shut his eyes. "God our Father, Peter Graham says You'll take care of him, so I give Seville into Your keeping. He's a bit mean and not very pretty, but I love him. And God, he likes the fish dinners best and the top of the milk. Thank You, for Jesus' sake."

"Amen." Peter squeezed Cass's shoulder. "He couldn't be in better hands."

"Do you . . . do you really think God's interested in cats?"

"God made them, and you told Him you loved Seville. God loves you, so of course He's interested in what you love. He's interested in every part of your life."

"Even when I cut my toenails?" It was the wildest thing he could think of.

"Even that."

"Well, thanks." Cass found it hard to believe, but Peter seemed to have no doubt about it.

Mrs. Leadbetter takes a boarder

CLARE WAS SO EXCITED on Wednesday morning that Mrs. Macken had to force her to eat her breakfast.

"I couldn't, Mum!" she objected when faced with a boiled egg and toast.

"You must, Clare. Come on, dear."

Clare bounced the spoon on top of the egg, then pushed the plate away. "Yuk!"

"No breakfast, no party." Clare laughed. Mrs. Macken didn't laugh in reply. The silence stretched on and on. Clare pouted, then pulled the egg back toward her. She took off the top carefully, sprinkled salt and pepper onto the exposed yolk and began to eat it too quickly.

"I'll be sick." It was a threat.

"All right. Eat some toast, that will help."

"I don't want it, Mum."

"Toast." Mrs. Macken's voice was firm.

"You're cruel, Mum. You don't want me to enjoy myself." Mrs. Macken left the kitchen. Clare looked miserably at her plate. She knew her mother wasn't cruel. She ate her toast, drank her orange juice, then cleared away her dishes. She wanted to go to her mother and say something that would show her she hadn't meant it, but felt suddenly shy.

"Carry your bag, Duchess?" Cass was bowing low and pulling at his hair.

"Yes, knave. Drop it at your peril!"

"Where is it, then?"

"Cass. You're cheating. You should say, 'Prithee, gentle maiden . . . .' "

"Well, prithee up, or you'll be late. This the lot?" Cass shouldered the bag and clattered down the stairs.

"Have fun, Clare."

"Thanks, Dad. Bye." Clare hugged her father. "Bye, Alanna. Bye, Mum."

"Good-bye, sweetheart. Have a lovely time."

Clare's heart lifted. Her mother was just as she always was. Cass was waiting for her downstairs. "You may kiss my hand," she said, holding it out and tilting her nose up as high as she could. The kiss was wet and loud. Clare snatched her hand away.

"Have a ripper time, Clare. And Clare . . . ."

"What?"

"Take care."

Clare laughed. "I'm only going with the class. After school."

"Never mind. Here's your bus. See you. And be careful." Cass stood and watched the bus out of sight. Then he looked up to the shop parapet, half expecting Seville to be up there sunning himself. There was no cat in sight. He turned round and saw Mrs. Leadbetter standing watching him from her balcony. Mrs. Leadbetter and . . . Cass caught his breath. O'Mara? What was O'Mara doing with Mrs. Leadbetter at this time of the morning? He went slowly inside.

"What's up with you, brother?"

"Alanna, what would O'Mara be doing at Mrs. Leadbetter's at this time of the morning?"

"He's boarding there, didn't you know?"

"Since when? Nobody told me."

"Didn't think you cared. Why shouldn't he?"

"It's too close," muttered Cass, half to himself. "She can cook all right, but his ears will suffer," he said aloud.

"He likes her."

"He's queer, Alanna. I wish he'd stay away from you."

Alanna only smiled. Cass was surprised she didn't flare up. "Different," Alanna said. "Not queer."

Mrs. Leadbetter, when she came in, gave no greeting but asked her question urgently. "How's she getting home?"

"Hello, Mrs. Leadbetter. I didn't hear you coming. Were you speaking to me?"

"Yes, of course I was. There's only you and your little brother here, and I wouldn't be talking to him, would I?"

Cass took the hint. He didn't want to get involved with her.

"Found your cat yet?"

Cass turned. "Not yet," he said evenly. "He's all right, though; I've given him to God to look after."

"If you're being cheeky . . . ."

"I'm never cheeky on Wednesdays, Mrs. Leadbetter." Cass walked away. Alanna's eyes were flashing danger signals at him.

"Well, poor lad, I guess he can't help it. Alanna, tell me, how is Clare getting home?"

"Mr. Vichelli is sending his biggest pumpkin on the stroke of midnight, with four white mice as footmen." Alanna spoke confidentially.

Mrs. Leadbetter burst out laughing. "You are a tease, 'lanna! I just wondered, that's all. It's a fair step, all the way from Castle Hill."

"What's at Castle Hill?" Adam had come in and heard the last sentence.

"What are you doing here so early, Adam?"

"I ran out of coffee, my dear girl, and all the shops will be shut by the time I get home tonight, so I came off the highway especially to patronize your establishment. And, perhaps, a little to say good morning to you. Now tell me, what's at Castle Hill?"

"Young Clare is going to a party there tonight. At Davenports'. I was just saying to Alanna, it's a fair step, and how's she getting home?"

"I'm sure Adam isn't interested in juvenile parties, Mrs. Leadbetter. Excuse me a moment." She gave Adam his change.

"Better if she stayed the night, if you ask me," Mrs. Leadbetter went on. "She could sleep in her panties."

"Why don't you go and suggest that to Mum?" Alanna was getting bored with the conversation.

"I just wondered. I didn't mean to push in. You don't mind me being interested, do you?"

Alanna pulled a face. "Of course not! Anyway, I didn't make the arrangements, so I don't know."

Mrs. Leadbetter nodded and wandered out. Alanna sighed and shrugged. She began talking to Adam.

A black Mercedes

"THERE'S A CAR HERE for Clare Macken. Clare? Get your things, my dear." Mr. Davenport smiled at the sudden shadow on the glowing face of his young guest.

"Who is it, Mr. Davenport?"

"Says he is Alanna Caterina's boyfriend, and he's driving a black Mercedes. Is that any help?"

"Oh, yes, that'll be Adam. I'll just say good-bye to the others." Clare went round the group, thanked her hostess and followed Mr. Davenport through the house toward the front. Just as they reached the door, the telephone rang, and Mr. Davenport excused himself and went back to answer it. Clare went on.

The door of the car was open, the engine running. Clare got in and had trouble with the string of her beach bag catching in the door, so she spoke before she looked at the man beside her. "Hi, Adam. Where's Alanna? Didn't you bring her too?"

The driver took the car between the high iron gates before turning on the lights. "Hi, Clare," he said.

It wasn't Adam.

After a while, Clare asked Vincent, "Did Adam lend you his car?"

"This isn't his car," the answer came shortly.

"Oh." Clare said no more. It looked the same car as the one Adam drove. She leaned her head back and thought about the party as the car swooped up and down the hills of the North Shore. Clare shut her eyes, pleasantly weary. She was almost asleep when the car stopped, and someone began undoing her seat belt. She sat up suddenly and cried out at the sight of the man who had joined the driver. He had a stocking over his face.

"Shut up!" he said roughly.

Clare struggled, flung her head sideways to escape the muffling hand and felt a sharp prick in her arm before she was overpowered and carried to another vehicle. She heard, very faintly, Vincent say, "Take her things."

Vincent watched the other car draw away. He swore loudly. Clare was a nice little thing; he hoped she'd be all right. Trevor had promised she'd come to no harm; that was part of the deal.

"How would you like to get Adam Spinks in bad with Alanna Caterina?" he'd said.

"Well, how?" In spite of his distrust of Trevor. Vincent couldn't help being interested.

"Clare's going to this party at Castle Hill, and I can borrow a black Merc for the night . . . no, listen! See, you drive up to this place and say you're Alanna Caterina's boyfriend and you've called for Clare Macken. She'll think it's Adam. Then you drive to Crows Nest and meet me. . . ."

"What's the point?"

"See, when she doesn't come home, they'll blame Adam because of the black Merc, and you'll be able to get in with Alanna Caterina again."

"Why? Do I find Clare and bring her home and come the big hero bit?"

"No, not quite. I'll handle that bit. But what do you say? You don't like Adam, do you? And the way he hangs around the Mackens is sickening, *I* think."

"What about Clare, though?"

"I'll just keep her at my place for the night. She'll be O.K."

"Why don't you do it yourself?"

"Clare likes you." Vincent knew that. "So does her big sister, really. She was more your way than my way before Adam Spinks shoved his oar in. How long since she's been out with you?" A green mist of jealousy clouded Vincent's mind. Alanna Caterina was his. She had no right to tease him going with other guys. As for Adam Spinks, he'd just better watch it. Him and his Mercedes.

"O.K.," he'd said to Trevor.

Vincent started the car and drove on. He'd ring Alanna first thing. He said her name softly. "Alanna Caterina."

His mind cleared as he drove along. What a sucker he'd been to believe Trevor! Why would Trevor want to help him, anyway? Trevor was in it for himself. "You poor nit," he said angrily to himself. "And that little girl—what's he up to?" He swung the car into a side street and doubled back to the highway. Well, whatever Trevor was up to, he wasn't going to get away with it, not if he could help it.

Vincent tried to remember all he knew about Trevor. It had been a big risk going to Davenports' in a black Mercedes. What if Adam had turned up too? Or Mr. Macken? Did Trevor know that they wouldn't be coming? And the Davenports, they wouldn't hand her over to anyone who turned up, would they? Trevor and the Davenports? Why? Vincent stopped the car outside Trevor's flat. It was worth a try anyway.

Trevor answered his door, annoyed at the interruption. He showed his nervousness, licking his lips and looking beyond Vincent to make sure there was no one else in the corridor.

"What d'you want? What're you doing here? I told you to take the car to . . . ."

"Cool it, man. Your boss says there's a change of plan. He wants her moved."

"Come inside. Keep your voice down!" Vincent stepped through into the flat. Trevor shut the door quickly behind him. "Now, what's up? What's it all about?"

"He wants me to take her from here. He doesn't think it's safe. Too much risk for you."

"Doesn't trust me, is that it?"

"You'd have your own reasons for thinking so!" Vincent's voice was an insult in itself. Trevor recovered himself.

"She's not leaving here without more authority than your say-so."

"No? So you have snatched her! That was a fine yarn you pitched me!"

"Only a sucker like you'd have fallen for it, anyway. Now get out, go on."

Vincent took a great deal of pleasure in punching Trevor on the jaw. Trevor hit the floor hard and stayed unmoving. Vincent found Clare in a bedroom and carried her down to the car. He went back for her things and on the way out dropped a dead flower arrangement on Trevor's chest.

Clare was still in a drugged sleep. Vincent shook his head. "Never mind, we'll soon have you home, Clare. Then I'll return the car, and that'll be finish with Mister Clever Trevor."

Everybody's night out

MRS. MACKEN WAS IN THE SHOWER when the phone rang. Alanna answered it. "Oh, yes, having a good time, is she? Good. Well, of course, I can see the point of that. I'll just check with Mum. MUM, IT'S MR. DAVENPORT. THE KIDS ARE ALL HAVING SUCH A GOOD TIME AND IS IT O.K. FOR CLARE TO STAY THE NIGHT AND GO TO SCHOOL FROM THERE TOMORROW?"

Mrs. Macken poked her head round the bathroom door. "As long as Mrs. Davenport can stand it, yes, why not? Does she want to have the extra bother?"

Alanna relayed the message. Mr. Davenport laughed. "No trouble," he said. "She'll enjoy it."

"Well, thanks very much, then. And give Clare our love. O.K. Bye." Alanna put the phone down. "She'll enjoy that, the dear kid. Say, Mum, why don't you and Dad go out? It would be a good opportunity, wouldn't it? And Cass has gone to that barbecue thing at the church. Go on, you might as well."

"What about you, Alanna Caterina?" Mr. Macken looked up from the paper he was reading.

Alanna laughed. "Oh, Dad, you're sweet!" She kissed the top of his head. "Did you ever know me stuck for a date?"

"You've got a point there. Who is it tonight?"

"Trevor. He's asked me to meet him in town."

"Not picking you up?" Mr. Macken was frowning.

"He's got to finish off something he's working on, and it

will be too late for the show if he has to come over here first.
I'll pop over on the ferry and he'll meet me at the quay."

"O.K. Sounds reasonable. Well, I'd better stir my stumps,
eh, Mother?"

From Mrs. Leadbetter's balcony, O'Mara watched the
lights go out above the shop. He waited another ten minutes
before he moved. For a while he'd wondered if his imitation
of Trevor in making a date with Alanna had been good
enough to fool her. He had to have time to search again,
he had to find his ank. His impatience over the resistance of a
couple of children fretted at his efficiency. Thakover, the
rendezvous time, was getting closer. He had to find it. Had to.

O'Mara was very thorough, very careful to put things back
exactly as they had been. In a matchbox, he could still see
the picture he had thrown up in Mr. Bywater's memory: the
convex disc in a handful of matches. His ank. It wasn't at the
hospital. The ambulance crew had not received it. It had to
be here, with the Mackens. He'd worked round Mrs. Leadbetter and Father O'Donovan, the Vichellis, Vincent, Trevor,
Peter Graham . . . there was nothing that brought him closer
to his goal. The Macken parents didn't know anything, nor
did Alanna Caterina. It had to be the boy, but the boy was on
his guard and suspicious. If Clare would relax, he could talk
to Clare; she was perceptive. He could get at the boy through
Clare; she was Cass's vulnerable point.

The doorbell rang. O'Mara hissed softly. He looked out the
window and saw the black Mercedes. Adam? He hesitated.
Vincent stepped back from the door and looked up at the
windows. He was carrying Clare. Clare!

Vincent stabbed at the bell again. The living area was in
darkness; only the night light in the shop glowed dimly.

"Hi, Vincent. What's up with Clare?" Vincent swung
round.

"O'Mara! I didn't hear you coming; you scared the daylights out of me. Clare? She's asleep, that's all. Too much party. I'm bringing her home."

O'Mara's eyes burned into Vincent's. He struggled helplessly against the will behind them. He obeyed O'Mara's directions and later had no memory of what he'd done or where he'd been. O'Mara's final instructions were that he should drive the car to where he'd been told to leave it.

Manipulating Vincent had taken power, but O'Mara was pleased with the night's work. Now he could rest for a while and then concentrate on Clare.

Clare woke up shivering. It was dark, and the air smelled damp. She couldn't think. Where was she? There had been the party, the lovely party, and the drive home.

She remembered now, the car stopping and the man undoing her seat belt and the pain in her arm and . . . .

The shudders started then, and the tears. Horrible racking sobs that didn't quite reach sound shaking her all the way through her body up into her throat. Arms crossed, hands clutching her shoulders trying to stop the panic, she stared round, looking for something to identify, something to dispel her fear.

A car engine roared. Clare sat still. There must be a street nearby. She listened intently. She could shout. Perhaps someone would hear. A faint roar and rumble approached, peaked, retreated. The bridge! A train on the bridge. She didn't know which side of the bridge. It could be close to home. She would believe it was close to home.

There were no other sounds for a long time, though Clare waited with held breath.

"Is anyone there? Hi! Can you hear me?"

Absolutely no response.

Clare thought about Cass. Should she call him? She tried to concentrate, then reminded herself that Cass would be asleep.

Perhaps she just thought she was locked in. Perhaps she could walk out.

Clare began to crawl over the floor. It was made of stone blocks; she could feel the joins and the roughness of the texture. When she came to a wall, she stood up and began to feel her way along. There was an angle, a long stretch of wall, another angle. Clare's foot slid into water. She gave a little cry and drew back. She explored the floor again with her foot. There seemed to be a shallow gutter. Bending down, she felt with her hand the shape of the gutter and the corroded metal grating through which the water ran.

The needs of her body became suddenly urgent. Propping herself against the angle of the wall, she pulled down her pants and cried as she emptied her bladder.

The gutter ran right along that wall. Clare followed it carefully. There was a faint moonshine high up. Enough to show thick bars in the shadow of the wall. After that, another stretch of wall before its evenness gave way to uncut rock. The water lazed its way down the rock; it was cool on her hands. She smelled it. Her nose told her it was sweet, carrying only earth and rock odors. The rock seemed to go right across one end.

Her hand touched wood. Clare drew in her breath. It was a stair. She found the bottom of it and felt her way up. Her head hit on something, and reaching up her hand, she could feel wood above her. It must be a trap door, she thought. She pushed. Nothing moved. She tried with both hands, then with her shoulders. The wood was unyielding. Slowly she went back to the floor level and continued her way along the wall. She stumbled over something on the floor and, reaching down her hand, found her beach bag.

There was no door, then. Only the one at the top of the stair. She picked up her bag and followed the wall back to the stair. She sat halfway up, leaning her shoulder against the bag.

God is.

The thought came to her from nowhere. She nodded her head. Nothing could alter that. Whatever else happened, wherever she was, *that* remained.

Weariness came in waves. Clare slept.

A dog barked. The sound came faintly as Clare woke up. She rubbed her neck and yawned. Sunlight the width of the barred window shone into her prison. Clare hugged her knees and looked all round, then up. The floor joists which formed the roof of her prison were dark with age, solid, uncompromising. She could just see the line of the trap door. A spider dropped down its thread in front of her face. Clare drew back with a little cry. The spider stopped, climbed a little, jerked down again. The girl's skin began to prickle. "Hi, spider. I'm Miss Muffett. Have you brought my curds and whey?" She said the words aloud, but could not hear them. The batteries in her hearing aid had given out. She fished round in her beach bag but could not find the purse containing her spare batteries. Without her hearing aid, it was still possible for her to hear some traffic noises or the barking of a dog.

Her bikini was still damp, so she hung it over the rail of the stair with the towel. A stained paper bag reminded her that she was hungry. Goodies from the party that she was taking home for Cass. The saliva ran into her mouth at the thought of food. No, she wouldn't touch it. They would be bringing her breakfast soon, and she would ask for some hot water to wash in. She needed to go to the toilet, too.

Clare began to shout.

It was no good, she couldn't wait any longer and the shouting only made her more desperate. Clare used again the corner where the water from the gutter escaped, hurrying in case they came with her breakfast, thankful for the mercy of the primitive water closet. Tears ran into her eyes. They could be looking at her and she wouldn't know. Habit made her wash her hands in the water channel, and she shuddered a little at the feel of the scum on it. Going back to get her towel, she dipped one end of it in the water and scrubbed at her face and neck. The coolness comforted her.

There was a pile of rubbish in the middle of the floor, broken wooden shelving, dust, rotting sacks, bottles. Funny, pale-cream toadstools grew out of the sacking.

Clare went round the walls again, thinking she might have missed a door. The corners were dim, but there was no door. The sloping rock down which the water trickled went back under the flooring. Clare wondered if she could climb up and squeeze under the boards. It was too dark to see how big the space was. She would shout first.

Standing back from the window, Clare shouted, using all the force of her lungs. On and on she went until she began to feel giddy. Her throat was dry.

"WHAT ABOUT MY BREAKFAST?" she screamed out. Then quietly, "Oh, I'd love a cup of tea."

There was a clean handkerchief in her bag. She took it and stood close to the rock, dabbing the handkerchief on the water trickle until it was wet. She held it in place and put a corner of the square in her mouth. The coolness soothed her. It was a slow drink, but it seemed she had plenty of time. She leaned her forehead against the damp rock and tried to think. There wasn't going to be any breakfast. They were going to leave her here. Forty days and forty nights Jesus fasted in the wilderness. She had water. Would she live forty days and forty nights? In spite of herself, the tears came.

"I'll eat Cass's goodies," she said aloud. "He won't mind. I'll eat some and then I'll call him." Choosing what to eat from the squashed mass took time. She ate a slice of sponge cake thick with cream, licking her fingers carefully and wiping the cream from the paper with care. There were two iced cup cakes and a large piece of fruit cake. And five jelly babies and seven Smarties. Clare ate two Smarties so that there would be five of each, then she had another slow drink. Her tummy rumbled.

She went back to sit on the stairway and concentrated on Cass. She couldn't reach him. "He must be angry about something," she thought and wondered what it could be. He was so different when he was angry. Was it because she hadn't come home? No, it couldn't be that because he would have been trying to reach her, too.

The long day stretched itself out, the light fading gradually. Clare washed herself, then her underclothes and hung them on the stair rail to dry. Anything to fill in time. She shouted. No one came.

When it was nearly too dark to see, Clare ate a cup cake and two sweets. The cake was dry and crumbly. She looked longingly at the fruit cake, moist and dark, but that was for tomorrow.

Sitting on the stair waiting, Clare was suddenly aware that someone was trying to communicate with her. "Cass!" she cried aloud, her mind going joyfully to meet his.

Only it wasn't Cass. It was pleased with her for thinking of Cass, it *wanted* her to think to Cass, it wanted her to tell Cass something.

O'Mara.

Clare shut her mind. She began to say her prayers aloud, concentrating on them, shutting O'Mara out.

"Mum!" she shouted. "Mum! Dad? Where are you?"

Two's company

CLARE ATE THE OTHER CUP CAKE for breakfast. She had decided what to do. After washing some of the dust off a bottle from the heap of rubbish in the center of the floor, she set it up where the light would fall on it. Next she put on her bikini and clawed her way onto the rock from the stair. It was damp and crumbly even where the water did not run.

Choosing the deeper space between two beams, Clare managed to crawl some distance along the rock. She felt spider webs and tried not to think that the spiders would get on her. She could smell decaying wood, the bitterness of age, the angry sourness of disuse. "Poor old house," she said aloud. "Poor, poor, poor old house."

O'Mara was trying to get at her again. Clare shouted. She shouted with all her might and banged on the wood above her head with her school shoe, which she had brought in case she met a nasty. All it did was bring down a lot of dust on her, making her cough.

Two little lights were shining, blinking. Clare watched them, unable to move. They disappeared, came closer, disappeared again. Clare banged on the wood with her shoe and shouted. The lights came more quickly toward her through cracks in the floor. She tried to get away, but in the narrow space could not turn fast enough. Something furry was patting at her face, putting a foot through a knot hole in the

96

wood. Eyes blinked. Clare could not hear the frantic purring, but she could feel it as she put two fingers up through the hole onto the cat's body. "Seville?" It was a question. She wished it wasn't so dark.

Clare tugged at the wood. It wasn't rotten enough to give way. By banging at it with the heel of her shoe she finally got the hole big enough for the cat to squeeze through. He wove himself around her face for a short time then leaped across her and disappeared.

"Seville! Puss puss. Come back. Pussy pussy pussy!" Clare was inching herself back toward the blink of light shining on the bottle. She regained the stair, exhausted and filthy.

Seville had found the fruit cake. He crouched over it munching and growling and looking sideways at Clare. Clare had a moment's panic, then she laughed. "Poor old cat. What have you been doing to yourself?"

The cat was thin, with matted fur, one ear was torn, and he had a wound on one shoulder. Clare watched him eating the cake and waited until he had finished. Cautiously, the cat sniffed at a raisin that had become dislodged and separated from the cake. He sat up and began washing himself. Clare picked up the raisin and ate it. It was the most delicious taste she could ever remember. She watched the cat washing and remembered her own filthy state, so she got her towel and cleaned herself as best she could in the water from the gutter.

Seville finished washing and demanded love. Clare nursed him and petted him, cried a little, thinking how pleased Cass would be to know the cat was alive. Not very well, but alive. She rocked back and forth, longing for her family, finding comfort in the cat's warmth.

Every time she thought of Cass, O'Mara got at her. She wondered why, as she had wondered ever since she had been kidnapped, why her? What for? What did O'Mara want? She did not dare relax in case it meant harm for Cass. But why Cass? What had O'Mara to do with Cass?

Bywater. O'Mara had made her say it over and over. Bywater! Now she was really by water! It was a thin joke and Clare did not laugh. Had the man given Cass something? Was that why there had been so many odd things happening? How could she send a message to Cass without O'Mara getting at him?

Seville.

"No!" she said aloud. "I need him here."

Seville was asleep in her lap, warm and companionable and close. She *must* be near home. The thought of being alone again was more than she could bear. She stroked the warm body in her lap. Seville did not stir. But the more she thought, the more obvious it became that Seville was the only answer. If she could get Seville out, he would go home. He must have gotten trapped where he was or he would have gone home before.

She slept.

The cat jumping off her lap woke her. He was stalking a cockroach. Clare had known they were there, seeing them scuttling into the darkness when she came upon them. Seville caught one and ate it. Clare felt her own hunger. She ate a jelly baby.

Sadness weighed her down. It was such a physical burden that her limbs felt heavy and she was reluctant to move. Reason strengthened her will. She must get Seville out somehow. The trap door was still tight shut. Clare tried again to move the rusty grating in the gutter but could not budge it. She was glad. She had tried, she had, but Seville would have to stay with her after all. A shift in the light pattern drew her eyes upward.

The window. But it was so high!

Clare took one of the batteries from her hearing aid and rubbed it over the mossy part of the rock, then wrapped it in a scrap of paper from the cake bag. She slid the package under Seville's flea collar and bound it in place with a shoe lace. It seemed firm enough and the cat didn't mind; he was used to her dressing him up with ribbons.

Stirring round in the rubbish heap with the bottle, the girl found two pieces of broken stone. She heaved one at the window. It hit one of the bars and lobbed on the wide sill.

Clare was panting. She *must* hit with the next one. She spat on the stone and muttered over it, then threw. Glass flew.

"Ha!" Clare picked up the cat and took him close up against the wall under the window. "Look, Seville, you can get out, up there, see?" Seville struggled out of her arms and leaped down onto the floor, where he wound himself round her ankles. Clare picked him up and tried again, holding him up as high as she could above her head. Seville did not understand. He stalked a cockroach and ate it. He was wary now of Clare and would not let her get close to him.

The girl went back to her seat on the stair. After a long while, the cat came to her. Clare petted him, talking to him. Seville settled down in her lap. Clare knew what she must do. She had been too confused to work things out properly the first time. It had been stupid of her to expect the cat to leap out of her hands onto the window ledge. She talked to Seville, stroking him. "You're my only hope, Seville. I want you here, but if you don't go home, Cass will never find me. He'll use his nose on that battery . . . he'll know. So you be a good cat. I've got to throw you, puss. Now, it won't hurt."

Clare got up, still nursing the cat, and walked over toward the window. She took Seville by the scruff of the neck, as a cat does her kittens, and by the tail, close up to his body. The vet had taught Cass to handle him so. Seville's body was rigid and helpless. She swung him back and forth until she felt she had the right momentum, then flung him toward the light. He touched the wall, scrabbled madly, was there.

"I'm sorry, Seville. I'm sorry. I had to. Go home, Sev. Home to Cass. Go on. Shoo!"

For a long time, the cat sat where he was, half-crouched, tail lashing. Then he vanished.

Clare wept. The loneliness was awful now that Seville had gone. The dark corners of the cellar were closer, surely they were closer? Even as she looked, they slid toward her, boxing her in. O'Mara was getting at her again. She would not let him into her mind. She would not.

Clare sang. Her voice was raspy and wavering, but she could not hear it. She sang all the Saturday night songs she could remember, one after the other without a break. She was tired. "Thank you, Jesus," she crooned, over and over, one of the choruses Peter Graham was teaching them. It was easy to sing, the notes falling gently into place in her mind.

She couldn't remember going to sleep, but she woke up with a smile on her lips because she had been dreaming she was home. They were all there—her father and mother, Alanna Caterina, Cass, Father O'Donovan, the Vichellis, all so pleased to see her. And Mrs. Leadbetter.

No! No! Not Mrs. Leadbetter. She didn't want Mrs. Leadbetter there! Clare panicked.

And, at last, O'Mara reached her.

It wasn't a demand O'Mara was making in Clare's mind. He seemed to be asking for understanding. This was too much for Clare; her compassion admitted his need for communication.

The landscape he was showing her was vast, uncluttered, sparsely dotted with herbage that suggested aridity. The small bushes grew out of lion-colored rock over which Clare walked with no feeling of harshness coming through into her feet. The temperature was pleasant, the light gentle and surrounding.

O'Mara put no pressures on Clare but left her to explore.

A small rise blocked the forward view, so Clare followed the slope to find out what was beyond. A track took her round the shoulder and onto a flat ledge. Beyond the ledge was a chasm, but filling the whole of her vision were mountains of almost uniform size on either side of a valley. There was no vegetation on the mountains that Clare could see; they were clothed with color. They glowed with bars of red, gold, orange, yellow, that merged and separated and merged again as Clare stared. Tears came to her eyes at the sheer beauty. She could stay forever watching the glowing rock.

Following the ledge around, Clare found more mountains. The place where she was seemed to be a mesa, very high up, because the distant bluffs were at eye level, the mountain roots hidden deep in the valleys below them. Eagerly now, Clare explored, climbing up another track onto the plateau. There were no mountains on this side, the plain stretched away to tawny distance, but on the right was a bright navy blue sea capped with white foam.

A long, low building claimed Clare's attention. There were birds flying around it. Birds? Clare nodded as if in confirmation. Her drawing of O'Mara had been right; they were very small people. O'Mara was explaining their flying suits, showing her the energy units, the locking transistor-type button that was like the ignition key of a motor vehicle. Clare looked at the button, interested but puzzled. It was about the size of a penny, slightly convex, heavy, smooth, opaque, a steely gray blue color.

Relaxed after her dream of home, still in a dazed delight over the colorful landscape of O'Mara's country, Clare was off her guard. O'Mara explored her knowledge of Cass and his affairs with utter ruthlessness. There was nothing; she knew nothing about it.

When he had finished, Clare tried desperately to claim O'Mara's attention on her own behalf. "What about me? What are you going to do with me?" Very faintly the knowledge came. She was only a means of getting at Cass.

Clare screamed and beat on the trap door with her fists.

How long can you make one jelly baby last?

Vincent turns nasty

ALANNA CATERINA WAS ON THE TELEPHONE. Mrs. Macken watched her with some amusement. Her elder daughter's face showed so clearly what she was thinking.

It had been a miserable, messed-up morning. Cass slept in and was grumpy about having to rush. He was missing Clare's bright face at the breakfast table and went off to school in a bad temper. Mr. Macken couldn't find his glasses and was already late when his wife ran them to earth in the back pocket of his best suit. Alanna Caterina was livid because Trevor hadn't turned up for their date. "It was so—so *humiliating!*" she stormed. "I waited and waited, beating off drunken sailors and dirty old men and expecting him to turn up every moment."

"Why didn't you come home, then?" Cass asked. "I wouldn't have waited if I'd been you."

"When he rang, he said he'd be there as soon as he could and to wait for him."

"Better luck next time," Cass said tactlessly. Alanna blew up, and her brother beat a hasty retreat. "I might be a bit late today, I'm going to have another look round for Seville after school," he called and ran off before anyone could say no.

Mrs. Macken had wanted to ring Mrs. Davenport. It was silly, she knew, but she was dying to find out how Clare had enjoyed the party. First one thing, then another had kept her away from the phone, the last straw being a mix-up over a soda delivery. And now Alanna was talking to Vincent.

"I can't, Vincent. It's very kind of you. . . . Yes, it sounds absolutely fabulous. . . . I know, but . . . it's got nothing to do with Adam having a Mercedes! I already told you, I've a date. . . . You can't tell me . . . . I'll go out with anyone I please, thank you!" She banged the receiver down.

The phone rang. "Wharf Road Supermarket, Alanna Macken here. Vincent, be reasonable! I can't spend all day on the phone. What? No! No no no NO!" Alanna Caterina stamped her foot. "It wouldn't make any difference if you had a polka dotted Rolls Royce with mink upholstery and a chime of bells, I can't break a promise. I can't go out with you tonight! . . . It's got nothing to do with you. Look, don't you try to threaten me. . . . What do you mean, I'll be sorry? No, I won't change my mind. Of course I'm fond of you, but I won't be if you keep . . . . Oh, drop dead!" Alanna hung up.

Mrs. Macken was trying not to laugh. She had her head down behind the counter. Alanna came round and bent over until she could look her mother in the eye. "Don't you dare!" she threatened. It was too much. Mrs. Macken went into peals of laughter. Alanna looked indignant, then laughed too. She shrugged. "No one's going to tell me who I can go out with," she said.

The telephone rang. "Would you like me to answer it?" Mrs. Macken offered.

"Please, Mum."

"Yes. Yes, she is. I'll put her on. Alanna—now don't look at me like that—it's Adam."

"Oh. Right. Thanks, Mum." The conversation was short. Alanna was laughing as she hung up. "After all that, Adam's off to New Zealand, so I could have gone out with Vincent after all."

"Sudden, isn't it?"

"Yes. He's chasing something up for a client, he says. Oh, well, I can always read a book."

"Better ring Vincent."

Alanna tossed her head. "What? You're joking! No way will I ring him. He'll kill me if he finds out, though. You won't tell, will you?" Mrs. Macken promised. "I hate jealousy. He was quite nasty, Mum. I was surprised. Almost threatening . . . ."

Alanna served a customer. "Wasn't it funny without Clare this morning?" she said. "She'll have such a lot to tell us when she gets home this afternoon. I do hope she had a good time; I'm sure she would."

"Of course she would have! I feel sorry for the teachers today; they'll have a giggly lot of kids. Elfina Davenport hasn't ever been a particular friend of Clare's, but I suppose if all the class was going . . . and Mrs. Davenport probably felt it was a long way for the child to come home. It gave us the chance to go out, too. We did enjoy ourselves. Your father can be quite mad at times."

"So that's where the others get it!" Alanna teased.

It was just before school was due out that Mrs. Davenport rang. Mrs. Macken answered the phone. "Clare left a little purse here last night," Mrs. Davenport said. "I've only just found it. It has her hearing aid batteries in it. Will it be all right if I send it with Elfina tomorrow to school?"

"Thank you, Mrs. Davenport. Yes, that will be fine. We have another lot here if she does need one tonight. It was so good of you to keep her there overnight. She would have been very tired . . . . What did you say? Mrs. Davenport, WHAT DID YOU SAY?"

"She wasn't here for the night, Mrs. Macken. A boyfriend

of her sister's came to pick her up. He was driving a big black Mercedes, Elfina said . . . . Mrs. Macken—you don't mean to say she didn't come home last night?"

When Mrs. Macken put down the phone her face was almost as white as her hair. "Alanna, what is Adam's phone number?"

"Why, Mum? Mum, what's wrong?"

"Adam called for Clare last night. She didn't stay at the Davenports' at all. Mrs. Davenport just found Clare's purse with her spare batteries in it and rang to tell me."

"*Adam? Adam* called for her?" Alanna's mind was racing. "Oh, no, Mum! It couldn't have been Adam. If he did, where is she?"

"Someone who said he was Alanna Caterina's boyfriend and driving a big black Mercedes." Mrs. Macken repeated the words unemotionally.

"But he's gone to New Zealand!"

"Ring him, Alanna. I want to talk to him."

"But . . . ."

"Hurry up!" Alanna dialed Adam's number.

"Adam Spinks, please," she said, trying to keep her voice steady. Then, "Oh, he's gone, has he? Just a minute." Alanna put her hand over the mouthpiece. "He's gone, Mum."

"Give it to me. Hello . . . ." Mrs. Macken's inquiries didn't get much further. "I spoke to Adam's father," she said to Alanna. "Adam didn't go out last night."

"But why would Adam want to kidnap Clare? Why would *anyone* want to? Mum, you don't really think it was Adam, do you? He'd never have rung me if he'd done a thing like that! You don't think he's taken her to New Zealand? Why, Mum? Why? Mum, what are we going to do?"

"I'm going to ring your father," was all Mrs. Macken said.

The shop was busy, and because Cass was late, it seemed as though every school child in the district converged on it. In the middle of the confusion, Mrs. Leadbetter appeared. "You are busy," she said cheerfully. "Where's that brother of yours?"

"Looking for his cat," Alanna said shortly. "It would happen like this, just because he's not around to be helpful." She raised her voice. "Now, look here, you boys, put the cover back on the freezer. If the polar ice melts, Sydney will be flooded. Make your choice and shut it up, O.K.?"

Mrs. Leadbetter helped herself to a cold drink. She watched Alanna dealing with the children, a gleam of amusement in her eyes. "You're efficient, Alanna, I grant you that."

"Thanks." Alanna's answer was distracted. "Look, is O'Mara home? Could you go over and ask him to come and give me a hand?"

"He went to Melbourne," Mrs. Leadbetter said. "Last night."

"Melbourne? He didn't tell me."

"Yes, suddenly." Mrs. Leadbetter was looking out the window and did not meet Alanna's eyes.

"Oh." Alanna dealt with another rush on sweets and drinks.

Cass came in, gloomily. He looked from Alanna to Mrs. Leadbetter and then at the confusion in the shop and didn't wait to change out of his school clothes. Alanna smiled at him, a tight smile. Mrs. Leadbetter watched them with avid curiosity. Cass avoided her and when the rush was past went into the storeroom. Still Mrs. Leadbetter waited, not trying to make conversation, keeping an eye on the door and watching everyone with bright inquisitive eyes.

"Oh, God," Alanna thought desperately, "she's waiting for Clare to come home!"

Mrs. Leadbetter buys up big

IT HAD BEEN AN AWFUL BUSINESS. Mrs. Leadbetter waiting like a crow over a weak beast, Alanna Caterina not knowing what was happening upstairs, Cass aware that something was wrong but keeping his end up in the storeroom. When Mr. Macken came home, Alanna thought he would close the shop, but after a quick word with her, he went upstairs.

"Isn't she coming home, then?" Mrs. Leadbetter could wait no longer in silence.

"Who, Mrs. Leadbetter?"

"You know very well who! Clare, of course. Isn't she coming home?"

"Of course she's coming home! Where else would she be going?" Cass answered quickly before Alanna Caterina opened her mouth.

"Bus is late, then."

"Sometimes happens."

"Well, I better get home and get tea on. I hope she's all right, after the party and all."

"Is there anything you want from the shop?"

"No. I just came over, you know, to hear all about it. Bye."

"Good-bye, Mrs. Leadbetter."

There was no time for Cass to ask questions. The shop was extra busy that evening. About half an hour before closing

time, Mrs. Leadbetter returned. "Back again?" Alanna remarked cheerily. Cass scowled.

"Found I needed some things," Mrs. Leadbetter said breathlessly. She took a trolley and began a slow promenade round
the shelves. "Where's your dad?"

"Upstairs, I think," Cass said. "Do you want to see him
about something?"

"No, no. Just wondered. He's usually in the shop at this
time." Cass went past on his way to get something

"Those are good," he suggested, pointing to a line that had
been hanging fire for weeks. "Real value there."

Mrs. Leadbetter muttered, "Is that so?" and put one in her
trolley. Cass grinned.

"There's a new line of cake mix, Mrs. Leadbetter. Of course,
no packet cake comes up to your cooking, but it's handy to
have a couple in the cupboard in case of emergency, don't
you think?"

"Some of those packet cakes are O.K. I always dress them
up, of course. A bit of extra salt, or some almond essence to
kill the taste of the imitation essences they use. 'Always use
pure essence,' my mother told me. 'It doesn't pay to use
cheap imitations and ruin good ingredients.' She had a lot of
common sense, my mother."

"That's where you get yours from, I'm sure," Cass flattered.
Mrs. Leadbetter simpered. Cass could feel the anger rising in
him and stamped it out quickly. He watched Mrs. Leadbetter
out of the corner of his eye and found her watching him. He
grinned at her and she moved on, adding more things to her
trolley.

"What are you up to, Cassowary?" The boy looked up. Father O'Donovan was waiting in the queue at the check-out.

"Nothing but good, Father. How's the bait tin?"

"Half-full or half-empty, I'm trying to decide which. You'd best come round and help me."

"Going fishing, then?" Mrs. Leadbetter came past with her trolley.

"Oh, hullo, Mrs. Leadbetter. How's the rheumatism? O.K.? That's fine. Are you stocking up for a siege?"

Mrs. Leadbetter looked at her trolley, then at Cass standing there with a half grin on his face. "Just a few things I need. You run outa things all of a sudden. I've just thought of something else." She pushed the trolley ahead of her down another aisle.

"And how did Clare enjoy the party?" the old priest asked Alanna Caterina as she checked his purchases.

"I haven't seen her yet to ask," Alanna replied cautiously.

"Oh?" Father O'Donovan was puzzled. "I thought she'd have come through the door beaming all over, surely?"

"SHE HASN'T COME HOME." Mrs. Leadbetter trumpeted the information from the back of the shop. "NO SIGN OF THE BUS, I'VE BEEN WATCHING. . . ." Her voice trailed off, as if she'd realized she'd said too much.

"Nearly closing time, Mrs. Leadbetter."

"Is it that late, 'lanna? Just gotta get a couple more things. Wouldn't want to keep you waiting." She put two more jars of the slow seller in her trolley and wheeled it up to the check-out. Father O'Donovan slipped round to the stairs and went up, giving Cass a quick nod as he passed.

"Bring a carton, please, Cass," Alanna said, waiting for Mrs. Leadbetter to find enough money to pay for her purchases. "And you'll have to carry these over; Mrs. Leadbetter will never manage them on her own." Cass muttered under his breath. Alanna frowned at him.

"I could make two trips." Mrs. Leadbetter's voice was eager.

"We couldn't think of it, could we, Cass?"

"No, Alanna. We couldn't bear to think of it, Mrs. Leadbetter."

"I'll carry the eggs meself if you can manage the rest."

"You must be going to do a lot of cooking, three dozen eggs! Here, I'll put them in a carry bag."

Mrs. Leadbetter nodded her head. "Having a boarder . . . ," she explained

"Then you'll be well stocked up for when he comes back from Melbourne."

"What? Oh, yes, yes, I will, won't I? Thanks, 'lanna. Come on then, Cass, don't stand around." Alanna watched them cross the street, served a late customer, who dashed in as she had her hand on the door to close up, then as soon as she could, ran to join her parents upstairs.

Cass staggered up to Mrs. Leadbetter's door, his mind on other things. Today the woman made him uneasy, somehow, whereas usually she just made him angry. He got the feeling that Clare was close, but just as suddenly she became distant, as if she didn't want his contact.

Mr. Leadbetter was feeding his birds, talking to them, to himself, and loudly to O'Mara. The aviary was on the balcony. O'Mara's door was slightly ajar but closed gently as Mrs. Leadbetter told Cass to put the carton down on the kitchen table.

"Is that you, Roseanne? Where's me tea, then? What took you so long?" He came into the kitchen, the packet of bird seed still in his hand. A thin man with a magnificent head of brown hair, waved and beautifully kept. He stared at Cass, who stared back. "Well, young Macken, put it down, then, put it down. No use hanging about here, you won't get anything however long you wait."

Cass turned and went. The boy heard his voice as he ran

down the stairs. "Spoiled brat, that one, eh, Roseanne? I was just telling our . . . ."

"Finish your birds, Art. Tea'll be ready in a jiff." Mrs. Leadbetter's voice drowned her husband's.

Cass went in through the yard gate, using his key, and up the outside stair. One look at his mother's face as he entered the room was enough to drive away all thoughts about the Leadbetters. He looked to his father, who was also pale, and Alanna crying into Father O'Donovan's shoulder. "What's happened?" the boy demanded. "It's Clare, isn't it? What's happened?"

"She wasn't at school today, Stewart." Mr. Macken spoke carefully. "She didn't stay at Davenports' last night, after all. Elfina says a boyfriend of Alanna Caterina's came to collect her in a black Mercedes. But Adam is in New Zealand, his firm says, and . . . ."

"O'Mara's in Melbourne," Alanna raised her head and dabbed at her eyes.

"He's not, you know. He's over at Leadbetters' now."

"Perhaps he just went for the day, Cass." Mrs. Macken always tried to be fair. "He went last night, he could be back now."

"What about Trevor? It was him stood you up, wasn't it, Alanna?"

"Trevor hasn't got a black Mercedes, as you well know. And anyway, he was working. Dad's checked with his office."

Cass's brain seemed crystal clear. "Adam doesn't own that Mercedes," he said. "It was hired, he told me. So anyone could hire a black Mercedes, couldn't they?" He looked round at the people in the room. "*Anyone.* And they could say they were Alanna's boyfriend. . . . Goodness knows, she's had enough."

"You shut up!" Alanna screamed.

"Now, now, children!" Father O'Donovan's mild voice brought them back to sanity.

"She wouldn't have gone with anyone she didn't know. I'm going to ring the police." Mr. Macken reached for the phone. "Stewart, have you tidied up downstairs? Then get it done, son, so we'll know where we are. Go on. You can't do anything by sitting round with a long face. Alanna, have you checked the till? And Mother, we could all do with a cup of tea, I think."

Cass cleaned up the shop mechanically, following the routine without thinking about it, his mind desperately exploring the possibilities of Clare's disappearance. Putting away the broom in the storeroom, he wondered suddenly why she hadn't called him. She always called when she was in distress. He sat on a carton of powdered milk and concentrated on calling her. It was no use. Each time he felt he was about to make contact, he ran up against a block.

"Father O'Donovan's saying prayers for Clare's safety," Mrs. Macken told him when he came upstairs. "And I've rung Peter Graham, too."

"He'll tell you to be thankful she's missing and praise God for it." Cass spoke bitterly. "That's what he said about Seville. He made me give him to God, but I dunno if God's looking after him or not. It's so *hard*, Mum. I don't understand. How can you be thankful if something awful's happening to you?"

"I guess God can only work good out of awful things that are not His fault if you hand them over to Him. We're not to know what good is being done to all of us, Clare, too, through this. . . ." Mrs. Macken turned away to hide her tears.

"I'm sorry, Mum. I shouldn't have said that. God will look after Clare, won't He, Mum? Won't He?"

Three cans of cat food

In spite of his protests, Cass was sent to school next day. "There's nothing you can do, Stewart, and we'll let you know straightaway if anything turns up. Be sensible, don't make it harder for everyone."

Cass bit his bottom lip. "It doesn't matter about it being hard for me, I suppose?" he burst out. "I just don't count in this family!"

"That's not true and you know it. And you know Clare dotes on you."

"Yes, but where *is* Clare?" The boy rushed out of the room, and the bathroom door slammed. Five minutes later he emerged and muttered an apology. "And you will let me know if . . . ?"

"Promise. The very minute."

Cass said nothing to anyone at school about Clare. He was reprimanded several times for inattention, and each time the classroom door opened, his head flew up to see if it could be a message for him.

"What's up with you, Cass?" Rowdy asked. "Still broody over your old tom cat, are you?"

"Aw, shut up, Rowdy. I was just managing to forget about him."

"I know where you can get a kitten," Frosty offered.

"Don't want a kitten." Cass's voice was low. "Seville will come back."

"Wanna bet? I bet you . . . I bet you a packet of chips every day for a week he doesn't. What do you say?"

"You're on!"

"And I bet you a Coke every day for a week he doesn't." Recklessly confident, Cass said, "You're on, too!"

"QUIET!" The teacher's voice cut across the whispers. "Settle down in the back there."

Cass did some mental arithmetic and the total sum made him feel sick. "God, you'd better send Seville home or I'll be bankrupt," he muttered.

When school finished, Cass ran, waving to Father O'Donovan, who was making inviting gestures for him to stop, and arriving at the shop scarlet faced and breathless. Alanna Caterina shook her head at his unspoken query. "No news," she said.

"But there must be something. What about the car, are they checking on the car?"

"Yes, they are. They're checking everything and everyone. It could take a long time. Hurry up and change, Cass, you know what's ahead on a Friday. And it's in the afternoon papers, so . . . ."

"O.K." In a way the routine needs of the shop were a relief, keeping his mind off the banging at the back of his consciousness: *Clare. Clare. Clare.*

Mrs. Leadbetter panted into the shop and with only a nod to Alanna went straight to the section where the pet foods were displayed. She bought sunflower seed and three tins of cat food. Alanna raised her eyebrows as she rang up the items. Mrs. Leadbetter shifted uncomfortably on her feet and held out her hand for the change. She refused to meet Alanna's eyes. "In a 'urry," she said. "Art wants it right away. Gotta sick . . . well, I'm off. Ta, 'lanna." She turned back. "I've read it in the paper," she said, and ran.

"What did she want?" Cass asked from the storeroom.

"Bird seed and cat food. Funny, Mr. Leadbetter can't stand cats near his birds."

"*Cat* food?" Cass came out into the shop. The oddest thought came into his mind. It couldn't be possible! Could it?

Peter Graham blew in, a grin still on his face. He looked his question, and Alanna shook her head. "Is there anything I can do?" he asked, serious now.

"Keep cheery," Alanna begged. "It's nice to see someone smiling. Must have been a good joke."

"Moke the Soak. He swears he's heard astral voices. I thought he was on the wagon, too. Says they were hallelujahing like mad and praising Jesus. I think years on the grog have done something terrible to his brain as well as his liver. I'll come back after you've shut and have a word."

"Bye."

At last the carefree hands of the clock strolled to closing time, and the Mackens could relax their face muscles. Alanna patted her cheeks. "My face is sore from smiling. How's yours, Dad?"

"About like that," her father answered. "People are kind, but it's a strain. At least we were spared any more of Mrs. Leadbetter."

"After last night's order, she won't need anything for a fortnight," Cass growled. "Bird seed and cat food. Fantastic! Dad, can I clean up later? I've had a thought . . . ." He was out the door and running before his father gave permission.

"He's still worrying over that cat," Alanna said fretfully. "At a time like this!" There was a knock on the door. "We're shut," she said.

"It's only me, Alanna Caterina, darlin', and I've run out of tea. Could you lend me a bit?"

"Father O'Donovan, you should be ashamed! Just a pinch I'll be lending you this time, and the cup in your other hand wouldn't be for sugar, now?" She opened the door and the priest slipped inside. He hugged the girl and patted her shoulder.

"That's my girl, never a surly answer have I had from you in all your life. Is there any news?"

"No, Father."

"I can't understand it. Why Clare? There must have been a mistake."

"If it were that simple, Father, we'd be giving thanks."

"Give thanks anyway, my friend, it's the open door to God's heart." He looked around. "Where's Cassowary?"

Alanna shrugged. "Who knows? He said he'd had a thought and shot through." She hesitated. "I think it was about Seville."

"I tried to stop him this afternoon coming home from school, but he had that much speed on I doubt if air brakes would have pulled him up. I heard . . . ." He rubbed his chin doubtfully. "I heard that there was a cat yowling in the old Milson place. The information came from a doubtful source, but explore every avenue is my motto."

"Avenue, road, street, lane, close, and crescent—Cass has been on them all."

"I know, I know. The same informant reckoned the Herald Angels were practicing too, and Christmas isn't that close . . . but just tell Cassowary for me, will you please?" He watched Alanna putting notes into neat bundles. "I must get back for confession. Don't let the devil dent your faith." He nodded again and left them.

Cass had gone by devious ways to the back of the terrace

where Mrs. Leadbetter lived. She had such sharp eyes, he could not be sure she was not watching the shop. Where Kettle Lane ran between Harbor and Zig Zag Streets, there was a broken wall that gave access to the jungle clothing the face of the cliff. Every kid in the area had a den or a cubby carved out of the lantana. Drunks used it for sleeping off their jags, and the householders found it a convenient dumping place for excess rubbish. Cass worked his way along until he was behind Mrs. Leadbetter's and squeezed through a hole in the fence. He crouched under an oleander with the uneasy feeling that he was trespassing. Now that he was there, he didn't quite know what to do next.

"Puss puss puss. Fishy dinner, pussy. Come on, puss puss." Mrs. Leadbetter's voice! "Can you see him, Art? He was there a bit ago."

"I dunno why you bother. I don't want him near me birds."

"I feel sorry for them, that's all. And O'Mara'd like me to keep him. Puss puss. Look, there he is on the flat roof of the old dumpty. Puss puss puss." Cass craned his neck. He could just see the patch of ginger. It had to be—it was—Seville!

"Look out, Roseanne."

"Art! What's come over you, you've made me drop the saucer."

"You're not feeding him. Not on my money, you're not. Cats! Here, look out, I say." Mrs. Leadbetter gave a cry and stepped back onto the saucer.

"Art! No!" Mr. Leadbetter took no notice. He seemed to have been seized by a frenzy and was hurling the ornamental stones from his wife's pot plants onto the roof where Seville lay. The cat crouched lower and lashed his tail, then a piece of brick caught him, and he jerked and lay still.

Cass gave a great shout. "Murderer!" he screamed, and

raced across the yard. He dragged a box close to the building, clambered onto it, scooped up the cat and ran.

When he burst into the living room, the limp cat in his arms, Cass was crying and shouting at the same time. "You found him! Is he all right, son?" Mrs. Macken went across to touch the matted fur. Her eyes were red from crying. "Where was he? He's been in a terrible fight by the look of him. Father O'Donovan was in and said to tell you a cat was heard in the old Milson place. And angels, too!"

Cass took no notice. "Look at him, Dad. Is he dead? Can we get the vet?"

Mr. Macken took Seville and put him down gently on the table. "He's not dead—heart is still beating, but it's weak."

"I'll warm some milk." Mrs. Macken went out to the kitchen.

"Mr. Leadbetter was throwing stones at him. I'll . . . I'll kill him! I swear I'll kick his head off! Can you see if anything's broken, Dad? I'll sick the RSPCA onto him! I'll . . . ."

All the fight went out of Cass like air out of a balloon. He could hear Clare's voice saying "Keep it pale, Mack. Keep it pale." He tried to reach her, desperately, touched her mind for an instant before it closed to him, and was aware of O'Mara's probing. "TICKYTACKY YUMYUM!" he shouted, to the utter astonishment of his family.

"Do be quiet!" his father said sharply. His fingers were feeling the cat all over, searching for sore spots. "He's been in the wars, but I don't think there's anything broken. The stones probably knocked him out. He was never particularly beautiful, Stewart, and he'll be even less so now."

"I don't care, Dad. You don't love people for their looks."

"He's only a cat, not a people." Alanna spoke sharply. "You should be worrying about Clare."

"Clare's all right," Cass spoke confidently.

"How do you know?"

Cass pulled at his hair. "I just do know. I don't know why or how. She's alive, anyway. I'm sure of that."

Mrs. Macken came in with the warmed milk. "I put a drop of brandy in it," she said. "Is he strong enough to drink it?"

Cass dipped his finger in the milk and ran it along Seville's lips. A rough tongue licked at the moisture. The cat sneezed, lifting his head. He explored the saucer of milk with his nose, then began to lap. A hard wheezy purr broke the silence. Mrs. Macken wiped her eyes. "Will you get that!" Cass spoke wonderingly. "He's half-dead, but he can still purr!"

"Bring his box up from the laundry, Cass, and I'll put a hot water bottle in it. He can sleep in your room tonight, O.K.?"

"Gee, thanks, Mum!" Cass went racing downstairs to get the box.

"He seems so sure. Do you think he knows? That Clare's alive, I mean." Alanna Caterina lay back in her chair, desperate for the hope to be confirmed.

"Clare and Stewart have always had a very close relationship, Alanna. She depends on him for so much—too much, I've thought sometimes. I think they share a bit of ESP."

"Then why can't he find out where she is?" Alanna asked tartly. Cass came back with Seville's box.

"Are you talking about me?"

"Yes. If you know Clare's all right, why can't you find out where she is?"

"Because O'Mara will get us if I try. She won't let me reach her. He tried to get me just now, that's why I yelled 'Ticky-tacky Yumyum.' It throws him."

"You're mad! You've got a thing about O'Mara. Anyway, he's in Melbourne."

"He's in Leadbetters'. I betcha anything you like he never went to Melbourne."

"Then why hasn't he been over, eh?"

"Stop it, you two. We've enough on our minds without you dragging O'Mara into it."

One jelly baby

CLARE WAS HUNGRY. She was thinking of all the delicious meals she had eaten. It kept the saliva running into her mouth but did nothing about the ache in her stomach. She had one jelly baby left. A hundred times she had resisted the temptation to eat it, although she had licked it. It was a red one. "When they come to get me out, I'll eat you," she said to it. "Just to show them." She wasn't sure what it would show them.

Tentatively, her mind reached out toward O'Mara. There was no response. She thought of Cass and made contact. Immediately, O'Mara seized on the contact and Clare shut him out. She cried. She wasn't going to be the means of him getting at Cass. She must be strong, she must.

Sitting with her knees tight up against her middle, hands clasped round them, she thought about her life. She realized that this was the first time she had ever had to cope with anything alone. There had always been the surrounding love of her family to cushion her. And Cass was special. She remembered the way he had come so quickly when O'Mara was hounding her. Dear Mack! She probably needed him more now than at any other time, yet she did not dare call him, and even if she did, she could not tell him where she was.

She wondered about Seville. Had he gone home? She had no way of knowing how high the window was from the ground. Or whether Seville had been hurt when she threw him. She shuddered just thinking about it. "I had to do it, Sev. I *had* to." Had Cass found the hearing aid battery? Had someone else found it first? What if O'Mara . . . ? She thought about something else quickly. She began to sing again.

A big cockroach scuttled across the floor. Clare rocked herself back and forth, watching him. He was fat. Seville had eaten a couple. What would they taste like? She shuddered. She wasn't that hungry—yet. It approached her, feelers moving, stopped, advanced. Clare stamped her foot. The cockroach sprinted straight toward her. Clare screamed and leaped to one side, shaking with the effort. The cockroach disappeared. Clare went to the place on the rock where the water dribbled down and drank and drank. She leaned her head against the cool dampness. "Thank You for the water," she whispered.

The dark came down and the walls closed in. Clare said her prayers but could not sleep. What if the cockroaches came out and began to nibble at her before she was dead?

Green moss

SEVILLE SLEPT, WOKE, ATE THE FOOD provided for him and slept again. Mr. Macken advised Cass to leave him alone until the cat showed signs of returning strength.

"I'm going over to see Mr. Leadbetter," Cass announced during a lull in the Saturday morning rush. "I'm going to tell him . . . ."

"You won't, Stewart. You'll stay right where you are, and under no circumstances are you to say anything to Mr. Leadbetter."

"But, Dad, he could have killed Seville!"

"Yes, or Seville could have been run over, or drowned, or struck by lightning. Just forget it, son, we've other things to do." Cass retired to the storeroom, muttering under his breath, and then was required to carry an order to Iona Avenue for an elderly lady. She was very lame and walked so slowly Cass thought it would be dark before they got to her flat. It was such a relief to be free that he ran all the way back to the shop.

Mrs. Leadbetter was there, waiting for him. "Ha," she said. "There you are."

"Yes." Cass was frozen faced.

"I wanted to explain," she tried again. "About the cat. My Art had a kind of seizure. He's not cruel. Got a real lovely nature. Wouldn't hurt a flea, he wouldn't. It was like some-

124

thing got into his head, he said, that made him want the cat dead. Couldn't help himself . . . ."

"Yes," said Cass again. "O'Mara probably." He turned away.

Mrs. Leadbetter looked as if she'd been hit in the wind. "Well," she said. "Well . . . ." She almost ran out of the shop.

After lunch, Mr. Macken called his son aside. "I want a word with you, Stewart. What's all this talk about O'Mara?"

Cass found it hard to start, but once he did make a beginning, the words just tumbled out of him. At first, Mr. Macken listened intently, but as the list of suspicions lengthened, he made an impatient gesture. "It's absolutely incredible," he said at last. "Just tell me one good reason why I should take you seriously."

Cass felt his anger and frustration coloring his face but he controlled his voice. "You don't believe me, then?"

"I don't feel like taking that story to the police, Stewart. Not unless you can produce some proof."

"What about him getting into the place when you'd locked the door? And Seville—he always acted funny when O'Mara was around."

"There's nothing tangible, son. Is there? Honestly?" Father and son looked at each other, the worry and grief of Clare's disappearance plain on their faces. "Anyway, you can bet the police will be interviewing him as soon as he gets back."

"But . . . ." The protest died on Cass's lips. Mrs. Leadbetter had got herself on TV as a "family friend," and her revelations about the Mackens made the boy squirm every time he thought of them. The dear, unfortunate girl, her devoted parents, her beautiful sister with strings of admirers—one of them boarded with her, yes, but was away at the moment—and the little boy and his lost cat. *Little!* It would give you the sicks, Cass thought, the old trout. He didn't believe O'Mara had ever gone away, he was motionless in his room like a spider waiting to trap an unwary fly. He wished his father had allowed him to speak to the reporters; he'd have told them a thing or two about the family "friend"!

The telephone rang. The police were sending a car; could the Mackens go with them to Castle Hill?

Cass was left at home with Alanna Caterina. It was no good trying to talk to Alanna; she wouldn't listen to a word against O'Mara. Cass went to his room and found Seville awake, stretching and yawning in his box. The boy knelt down, stroking the matted fur. Seville began to purr and made a few tentative licks at his coat. "Poor old marmalade," Cass murmured. "You are a mess. Here, I'll take your collar off and you can have a proper go at yourself."

The fur was matted and tangled round the collar. Cass worked patiently to get the fur straight. "Hello, old feller, where did you get the shoelace? Eh? Wish you could talk, you old fireball." He unwound the lace and gave a grunt of surprise when the small package fell out. The brown paper had almost worn away where it had been moist. Cass sat back on his heels and stared at the small round object in his hand. "Clare!" he whispered. "Oh, *Clare!*" He sprang up and ran into the living room. "Alanna, Seville has been with Clare!"

"You're mad. Mad and cruel . . . what's that? Show me!" She stood over him, reaching out to grasp the hearing aid battery in her brother's hand.

"It was wrapped up in paper under Seville's flea collar and tied up with a shoelace. Look." The boy held out the lace but kept the battery in his other hand. "Don't touch it, I want to see what's on it. It's been in something." He sniffed at it.

"You can't be sure it was Clare's . . . ."

"Who else would wrap up a battery and tie it round my

cat's neck? Alanna, it *has* to be Clare's. She's sent him to tell us . . . ."

"Is anything written on the paper?"

Cass shook his head. "I wish Dad was here. What do you think we'd better do now?"

"I'll take it up to the police station right now. Get an envelope and put everything in it. I'll call a cab . . . ."

After she had gone, Cass went back to Seville. He put him on a sheet of paper and brushed him all over, being careful not to hurt the sore spots. A small splinter of glass was in the matted fur round a cut. Cass put it in a jar and then rolled up the paper and put a rubber band round it. Seville was pleased with the attention and sat on Cass's knee, kneading his claws on the boy's leg. Cass picked up a paw and examined the pad. There was a trace of green moss between the toes.

Green moss!

Milson's place. Father O'Donovan had said to tell him a cat had been heard there. And angels—singing!

It didn't occur to Cass to leave a note. He dropped Seville back in his box and went running.

The old Milson place

WHEN CLARE WOKE UP on Saturday morning, she was giddy from hunger. The red jelly baby tantalized her, and she licked it twice before putting it away again. She washed herself carefully, taking a long time. Anything to help the day go. The heap of rubbish that had been in the middle of the floor was now mostly concentrated under the barred window. Clare threw anything with any weight, trying to get it through the bars so that someone, anyone, would notice.

The hope that she would be released was fading. She knew that O'Mara had neither pity nor compassion. All his efforts were self-directed.

Clare got really mad. "All right," she shouted. "All *right*. I'll get out by myself, see!" She climbed up onto the rock face and wriggled along to the hole where Seville had come through to her. Lying on her back, she began to bang at the edges with her school shoe. It was tiring and she had to take frequent rests, but she worried away at it, pulling off the bruised wood in long splinters, spitting the falling dust out of her mouth. Her shoe was breaking apart; she would have to go back for the other one.

Down in the center of the floor she sifted through the rubbish once more, looking for a lever or anything solid enough to bang with. The old shelving was as rotten as damp and age could make it, and she had used all the bits of stone or rock as missiles. The end of a bottle caught her eye. Perhaps it would work better than her shoe, but she would have to be careful of the jagged edges. She took it and her other shoe back up onto the rock.

When Clare got to the hole, there was suddenly no incentive to work. She lay on her back, looking at the smallness of it. She began to sing in her tuneless voice the chorus whose notes should have fallen as easily as water dropping down over stepped rocks: Hallelujah, thank you, Jesus.

Above her in the abandoned house, the vagrant who had told Father O'Donovan he'd heard angels and cats had just taken a fresh bottle of metho from its wrapping. He banged at his ear with the side of his hand, but still the singing persisted. Taking the bottle with him, he followed the sound.

Clare stopped singing. She looked again at the hole above her and did some scraping with the end of the bottle, but it was too slow. Anger burned up in her and she began to shout and bang with her shoe. She could not hear the startled cry of terror or the crash of breaking glass, nor did she know about the match held to the cigarette that dropped from the trembling fingers of the vagrant as he fled.

Clare stopped banging. She could smell fire. She lay very still, concentrating on what her nose told her. A wisp of smoke eddied along the floor above her and oozed through the hole she had made. Clare retreated, coughing, shouting as she went.

O'Mara. She had to reach O'Mara. He couldn't burn her! He couldn't! There was no contact.

Cass! Cass! Cass!

He was coming, she knew it, and she cried with joy.

Cass, running toward the old house, heard her call and responded. The fact that O'Mara broke into his mind was unimportant. The small, round, opaque convex object that O'Mara projected into his inner vision did not mean a thing to Cass. He had never seen it. He concentrated on Clare, the breath sobbing in his throat.

He smelled the smoke before he could see any sign of fire. Skidding down the slippery path at the side of the house, he wondered how he would get in. The doors and windows were securely boarded up, as everyone knew. They'd tried them often enough. Down past the main entrance, round the bottom end of the house and up the other side, the boy ran. There was broken glass and a pile of rubbish outside the barred window of the cellar. Cass hesitated. He heard Clare's shout and her school shoe, the broken one, came flying out almost at his feet.

"Clare! I'm coming! Hold on, Clare!"

Clare could not hear his shouting. Father O'Donovan in the street above did. The vagrant had rushed babbling to him with more talk of singing and banging from the Milson house. The priest had asked him to come and show him, but the vagrant refused to return. Under pressure, he told the old man how to get in. "Cassowary! Wait for me. I know how to get in!" The boy heard and ran to meet his friend.

"She's in the cellar," Cass panted.

"Round here . . . . Can you smell smoke? Holy Mother, the fool's set fire to the place. Look, me boy, behind this bush. There's a nail you pull out. In the shutter. Be careful now. I'll get the fire brigade. Wait here." He was gone.

Cass heard Clare shouting. He looked round. He could smell smoke, but there wasn't any coming out of the building yet. Clare's signal was loud and desperate. Cass slipped through the shrub-masked window.

It was dark inside the house after the brightness of the sunlight, and Cass stood still waiting for his vision to adjust. There was no sign of fire in this room, but his nose told him it was in the house. He hesitated. "Better not go rushing around," he said to himself. "She must be in the underneath, so how do I find that? It'll be on the other side of the house from here. Hang on, Clare, I'm coming."

The house was built on a T shape, and the French window through which Cass had entered was in the old dining room. A huge carved sideboard almost filled one side of the wall, the only piece of furniture left. It must have been built inside the room; there was no way it could have been gotten in through the doors or windows. Cass opened the door to get to the other side of the building. Smoke billowed, and flame, fed by the draft, flared out to meet him. He slammed the door, choking. A hatchway at the other end of the room led into the kitchen. Cautiously the boy pushed at the sliding door. There was wispy smoke but no flame here. He eased his way across the old counter, turning his shoulders sideways and pulling against the frame with his hands.

He could feel the heat now and the air was harsh in his lungs. One thought drove him on: Clare, trapped, frightened, needing him. He ran to the other end of the kitchen, past the big old iron range and the dusty butcher's block. A narrow passage took him to the entrance foyer with its circular staircase leading up to cobwebs, color from dusty stained glass lying gently where sunlight played on it between cracks in the boards on the high windows.

The smoke was thicker now and he could hear the flame gnawing at wood. With smarting eyes, he dashed across a hall billowing with smoke, groping for a door that had to be there. It took him a while to find it, and it was a sliding door that stuck and would not budge. Cass got his shoulder into the opening and pushed with all his might, shifting the door enough to get through. He could hardly see for the smoke and his smarting eyes. Now what? There must be a way down. There must be. He dropped down on his hands and knees and groped his way along the floor. Clare was shouting again, almost beneath his feet. There had to be a way down. There just had to be!

Frantic now, Cass scrambled round the floor, found the wall, followed it until he met a cupboard. Round that to the wall again. Nothing. Under his feet a steady banging began. "Keep banging, Clare. Keep banging!" It was a prayer. There was silence again except for the sounds of the fire. Cass was gasping, choking. Another bang. Near the cupboard. "*In* the cupboard, you fool!" the boy said aloud. He found the door, opened it and shut himself into darkness. Draft feeds flames, he kept thinking. Shut the doors.

He stumbled over something and felt rough edges under his hands. A piece of masonry. Grunting and heaving, he slid it along the floor. There was a ring let into the wood. Sweating, mumbling unintelligible words, the boy pushed at the stone. Every now and then he tugged at the ring bolt, but still the stone was on the trap. A sound behind him made him turn. The cupboard was alight! Frantically now, Cass worked at the stone and got it clear at last. He heaved on the trap door and tumbled into glare brighter than daylight.

"Clare! Clare!" he shouted.

Cass and Clare

CLARE WATCHED THE FLAMES eating away the roof of her prison and felt a rush of triumph. "Now I'll get out!" she defied O'Mara. Then the fear came and panic said, "You'll burn first."

Smoke hung above her, curled lazily toward the broken window and oozed out into the day. Clare coughed. She wet her handkerchief in the gutter and held it across her nose and mouth. "Towel," she thought. "Wet the towel." She rolled up her towel and laid it in the gutter to get wet. Down low, the smoke was not so bad. She crouched against the wall, watching. The walls were pressing in against her, drawing the fire right on top of her.

"No, no!" Clare shouted, sprang up and raced across to the stair. She banged on the wood of the trap door and screamed.

Cass! He was coming, she just knew he was coming. It quietened her for a while, and she half-lay on the stair, willing Cass to come. Then she began banging again. A section of burning floor fell into the cellar and sparks flew. Clare ran down the stair and across to where she had left her towel. She dragged it out of the gutter and put it over her head. The wetness was delicious on her parching skin. She lay down in the gutter as close to the damp rock as she could get, shuddering and hiccuping with terror.

Cass shaded his eyes from the glare. "Clare?" The burning wood in the middle of the floor was nearly consumed. The stone was cracking with the heat. Above him, the flames crept, masticating the wood with disgusting noises. A section sagged suddenly and hung, dropping torches onto the stone floor.

Was that she, that filthy bundle huddled against the rock? "Hang on!" Cass shouted and raced across and flung himself down across his sister's body as the floor above caved in.

Fire sirens wailed in the street. Clare heard them faintly, and felt and smelled the dear familiarity of her brother's presence. "Cass," she whispered hoarsely. "Oh, *Mack!*"

By Thakover

O'MARA SAT HUNCHED OVER in his room in the Leadbetters' house, fighting against the anger that threatened to drain him. After all that! Nothing. *Nothing!* He'd been so sure it had to be the boy. And now? He could hear the Senior's voice in the control room at the beginning of the mission:

"Now remember the limits. If you don't return by Thak-over, we can't wait for you. And if you lose your ank you'll have to stay on Earth . . . ."

To stay on earth with *people?* He hated people!

He went back over the possibilities. Could Bywater have tricked him? Had he hidden the matchbox before he had the heart attack? O'Mara shook his head. He was sure he'd picked up a flicker of power as he passed the Mackens when they were aiding Bywater near the shop. He controlled himself. Such thoughts would lead nowhere, and already he was feeling weakness attacking him. He had two more days to find his ank. Two days before Thakover, the deadline set by the Senior for the last possible rendezvous with the space platform.

O'Mara brought memory recall onto Bywater's recollection of the ank. It wasn't the ank that was so important to Bywater. He'd been surprised and pleased, but there was something else. All O'Mara could get was a feeling in the tip of a finger of something small and flat and round. Of course! Anxiety and impatience had made him blind. To him the ank was all important, but to the humans the ank was a nothing, a curiosity. Why had Clare been kidnapped? Not for the ank, for the other thing!

Vincent? Vincent was a lovesick, jealous fool. (O'Mara had learned of his deal with Trevor while Vincent was under his hypnotic spell.)

Trevor? Trevor was a different can of star dust altogether. Clever, hard, ruthless. Trevor wanted the other thing. Did they both work for the same boss? No, it was Alanna Caterina who had brought them together and chance had thrown Bywater down in front of the Mackens. Vincent wanted only the girl, but clever Trevor thought he could get both and was prepared to use Clare. O'Mara nodded. He understood Trevor very well. It was the man behind Trevor he had to find. He'd had Clare kidnapped to get what he wanted for nothing, but O'Mara had tricked Clare away. So now this man might have to bargain with Bywater. And whatever it was, the two things were together, that and his ank.

The wailing of fire sirens broke in on his thoughts, and then Mrs. Leadbetter banged on the door. "There's a fire!"

"I can hear the sirens."

"But it's real close. It's just up on Zig Zag Street!"

"Don't worry, Mrs. Leadbetter. You're safe down here."

"But it's Milson's place. All that scrub'n stuff, it'll rush down on us in a twinkling." O'Mara came out onto the back landing. Mr. Leadbetter was covering his birds.

"You gotta protect 'em from the smoke," he said, adjusting a sheet.

"There's plenty, look at it," his wife answered. "Just as well there's no one in the old house."

O'Mara remembered Clare. He tried to reach her but could not make contact. He shrugged his shoulders.

The police car dropped the Mackens outside the shop. "Wonder where the kids are?" Mrs. Macken said, looking round the empty rooms.

"Stewart will be up at the fire," Mr. Macken replied, "but it's hardly Alanna's cup of tea."

"Seville's here. He's looking better. Like a cuppa?"

"Good idea. We didn't get much further, did we?"

"No." Mrs. Macken filled the kettle. "I felt sorry for Mrs. Davenport, didn't you?" Her husband grunted. "She didn't seem to know all that much about him and his business, did she?"

"It's not every man who's blessed with a clever wife like mine!" Mrs. Macken pulled a face at him. It was funny how life had to go on, no matter what. We're taking refuge in the ordinary, she thought bleakly.

"She thought he'd gone to Japan, but his secretary said it was New Zealand. Extraordinary!"

"Adam has gone to New Zealand, too. Hello, here's someone coming home."

It was Alanna. "How did you go, Dad?"

"Nothing really. Like a cuppa?"

"You're very calm about it," Alanna said. She started to cry. "If there'd only been a message . . . ."

"What are you talking about?"

"Didn't Cass tell you?"

"He wasn't here when we got in. I suppose he's at the fire."

"Then you don't know?"

Mrs. Macken sat down rather suddenly. "Know what? Is there news? The police didn't . . . Alanna, for goodness' sake!"

"There was a hearing aid battery tied under Seville's collar with a . . . with a shoelace, and Cass said . . . Cass said . . . ." Alanna couldn't go on.

Her parents looked at each other, hope springing in their eyes. Mr. Macken put his arms round his daughter's shoulders and comforted her. "Where is it, Alanna?"

"I just took it straight up to the police. I didn't know what else to do."

"Good girl. Where's that tea? We could do with it."

"You two sit down, I'll get it." Alanna blew her nose. "The fire's in the old Milson place, did you know? I hope it burns to the cellar. It's been an eyesore for years."

Father O'Donovan puffed his way back to the old house after ringing the fire brigade. He'd tried to ring the Mackens, but there was no one answering. Cass was nowhere in sight, but the shutter over the French door swung wide. Then he heard Cass shout, and the crash as the floor caved in.

The priest was shouting through the cellar window when the first fire engine came, and got the men to direct their hose through the bars. "There're two children down there," he said pointing. "God help them."

"You sure about that, Father?"

"Absolutely."

"Right. Harry, hey, Harry! Coupla kids in the cellar." Training and discipline swung into action as the rescue was planned and executed. Father O'Donovan took Clare from the fireman who brought her up the ladder to safety.

"I've lost my jelly baby," she said. "It's a red one." She went limp in his arms. The old man carried her out of the way of the firemen and laid her down on the grass. Cass, hair and eyebrows singed, face blackened, shirt torn, found them there.

"Thank God, Cassowary!"

"Amen, Father. Is she all right?"

"I think she's fainted, and no wonder. Sit down here beside her, me boy, and get your breath. Easy now. I'll be back in two shakes of a lamb's tail."

If Mrs. Leadbetter hadn't been so busy watching the fire from her back landing, she might have seen Clare and Cass come home in a police car with Father O'Donovan, followed later by the doctor. O'Mara saw them, watching the procession with indifference. He had decided what to do—start again from Bywater.

Last lap

ADAM SAT ONCE MORE in the office of the managing director of the James Eve Company. It was Monday morning. A girl had brushed past him as he came from the outer office. She was crying.

"Sorry to keep you, Spinks. Everything happens on Mondays! That girl—you saw her? Been with us two years, held a position of confidence. She's just been telling me that she was offered a bribe to steal our new formula, but backed out at the last minute."

Adam whistled. "Honest of her to tell you," he said.

"Yes, I know. She's that sort of girl. That's why it seems so extraordinary. Point is, she's lost a microdot that has details of the superannuation and retirement entitlements of the whole national organization. Said she was in a hurry to get home and slipped it under the pad of her typewriter, and it wasn't there next day."

"When was this?" The managing director told him. Adam checked his notebook. "Hmm. The day before Bywater took his tumble. I guess she's been screwing up her courage to admit it. Is she by any chance romantically linked with Darren Pryse?"

"Who's he?"

"Cleaning staff. He met Bywater at Ball's Head Reserve that night. At the time I wondered . . . ."

Mr. Todd laughed. "It's very inconvenient for us, of

course, but I'd almost think it worthwhile if Bywater thinks
he's got the formula and instead has our Retirement Fund!"
Adam grinned. Mr. Todd glanced at his watch. "Now, how
did you go in New Zealand?"

"Got back early this morning. Had a seat next to Davenport of United Metals."

"Ha, did you, now? He's another who'd give his eyeteeth
for our process."

"Perhaps I could introduce him to Bywater," Adam suggested. He gave his report in detail and finished up by saying,
"Now what about the other business—O'Mara and so on?"

"Keep an eye on him still. And Bywater. I would like that
microdot back—if he's got it, that is."

"And Davenport?"

"No. We can't cover everyone. Anyway, Davenport's too
wily a bird to act directly. More likely to use one of his
subsidiary company men if he's in the market for anything."

"Right. I'll be in touch then." Adam got up.

"Thanks. It's a relief to have that New Zealand thing fixed."

"I'll get the report typed for you straightaway." Adam
went straight to his office and tried to ring Alanna Caterina,
but the phone was engaged. It was engaged every time he
tried. Exasperated, he dialed Complaints but could get no sat-
isfaction from them. He decided to go across to see her just
as soon as the typist had finished the James Eve report.

"They say the devil looks after his own," Mrs. Leadbetter
said sourly to Cass early on Monday. "It's a miracle how you
got out, that's all I can say. I said so to Art. 'It's a miracle,' I
said. How's Clare today?"

"She's fine. We're keeping her in bed for a while." Mrs.
Macken sliced Devon with a practiced hand. "Is there anything else?"

"No, thanks, not today."

"No cat food?" Cass dropped the question casually. Mrs. Leadbetter went a mottled red. The blush started on the tops of her arms and worked up her neck to her face.

"Just because you've got a scorched back and more praise than a trick elephant don't mean you can insult your friends," she sniffed. "Just be thankful you got your cat *and* your sister out of that house. The saints were looking after you and no mistake."

Cass shook his head. "No, it wasn't the saints," he said. "I reckon God did that bit of looking after Himself." Cass spoke seriously. Mrs. Leadbetter lingered, waiting for more information. "By the way, Mrs. Leadbetter, is O'Mara back from Melbourne yet?"

"No. Yes. . . . What do you want to know for?" Mrs. Leadbetter took her parcel and went off without another word.

"Do you have to do that, Cass?"

The boy shrugged his shoulders and didn't answer.

Mr. Bywater had made good use of the phone in his room at the hospital. He was sure that his possession of the formula was not known by the James Eve Company and was now anxious to sell it quickly. The time for a killing had come. Unisteel's representative had offered to pick him up at the hospital and drive him home. Whatsisname? Mr. Bywater searched his memory in vain. Trevor something or other. Once this deal was through, he could retire, and then it wouldn't matter any more if he forgot names or other things.

He dialed the number and asked for "Trevor . . . er," and got put straight through. "About four, then," he said at last. "I want to pick something up at Mackens' if you don't mind. Won't take long. Yes, that's right. O.K. See you then."

Trevor hung up. He'd had a bad day. Mr. Davenport had

put him on the mat about his bungling over Clare. He'd raved on about why should he alter his arrangements, and he certainly hadn't sent Vincent back to move Clare somewhere else. "You've got one more chance," he said. "I want that formula, is that clear? But for your inefficiency I could have had it for nothing." Trevor agreed that Mr. Davenport's instructions were clear. He tried to ring Vincent, but there was no answer. He'd been trying all day. Vincent had disappeared. Trevor shrugged off a niggling fear that Vincent might talk.

O'Mara fretted. There was so little time now. He no longer pretended that he wasn't worried. One small spark of hope remained. He'd gone up to the hospital to see Mr. Bywater and from outside his door had heard him on the telephone saying he wanted to call at the Mackens'. O'Mara hurried away and went back to take up his observation post on Mrs. Leadbetter's balcony.

On Sunday afternoon there had been a phone call for Cass. It was Mr. Bywater. "Look, son, I'm coming out of hospital tomorrow. I'll drop by and pick up that key ring . . . about half-past four. . . . O.K.?"

"Hang on," Cass said. "I'll ask." He covered the mouthpiece with his hand. "Dad, it's Mr. Bywater. He wants to know is it O.K. for him to call in tomorrow afternoon."

"Getting out of hospital, is he? Yes, tell him it's O.K." Cass passed on the message and hung up. His father was looking at him. "Why does he want to call in, Stewart?"

"Well, you see, Dad, I've got a . . . he gave me . . . you know when he fell over outside the shop? He asked me to mind something for him . . . ." Nobody spoke. Cass got the fidgets. "He said not to tell," he explained at last.

"And it's been here all this time?"

Cass nodded.

"Where?"

"Safe." Cass got a stubborn look on his face.

"Good to know we've a trustworthy son, eh, Mother?' Cass looked at his parents uncertainly. His mother nodded at him and smiled. The boy relaxed.

"Will you be glad to give it back, son?"

"Will I ever!"

That night, after Cass had gone to bed, Mr. Macken made a phone call. He explained why he had rung, then added, "So I thought you might care to drop by about half-past four tomorrow. O.K.? Right. Yes, I'll make it my business to be home. Oh yes, yes, we have a tape recorder. You think it's necessary? Well, you could be right. No harm done if there's no hanky panky and if there is . . . . Yes, you can say that again! We sure have had enough!"

The Mackens had stayed behind firmly shut doors all day Sunday, the phone off the hook. Clare, warmed, fed, and surrounded by the security of her home, slept. Cass nursed his scorched back and waited with what patience he had for Clare to be well enough to talk to him. Her interview with the police had worn her out. She did not mention O'Mara; she wanted to talk to Cass first. Now that she was safe, it seemed like a nightmare remembered from a long time ago.

The brass button

ADAM PARKED THE BLACK MERCEDES in front of Vichelli's, waved to Mrs. Vichelli, who was polishing apples on her apron before stacking them in the window, and headed toward Mackens'. Cass saw him coming, but Adam put a finger to his lips. Alanna Caterina was busy checking an order. Adam went straight upstairs.

Cass glanced at his watch and then looked up and down the street. He stiffened. Another black Mercedes slid to a stop behind Adam's. A man got out. Cass was not looking at the man, but at the dent in the hubcap of the rear wheel. In a flash, he was back on the footpath kneeling beside Mr. Bywater and looking up expecting the ambulance and seeing instead the big car slowing, then sliding smoothly past. He'd forgotten about that dent until this very minute. It was the same car! There had been two men in it that morning, he was sure, but Mr. Vichelli said there was only one man in the black Mercedes that morning. That was it, then! There had been two cars. Two cars in the street now, two cars that morning. His mother had sent Cass inside just as Mr. Vichelli came out and that was why they each thought the other wrong. He and Mr. Vichelli had seen two different cars. Cass went through into the storeroom to think things out.

From Mrs. Leadbetter's balcony, O'Mara watched Mr. Bywater getting out of the car. Soon now, soon, he told himself. There would just be time. He could swagger back to the platform at the last possible moment; no one need ever know how close he had come to missing the rendezvous. He moved quickly and silently.

Trevor locked the car and followed Mr. Bywater into Mackens'. "Stick close," the boss had said. Trevor didn't think there was any danger of losing the game now. He looked completely confident as he came through the door. "Hi, Alanna, sugar plum," he said. "What's new?"

"There's some aftershave and insect repellent if you're interested. Otherwise, nothing new, just the same old things," Alanna said briskly, trying to keep calm.

"You never change, just the same delicious tease," sighed Trevor.

Mr. Bywater was talking to Mrs. Macken. "I must thank you again for what you did for me," he said.

"It wasn't necessary to come in for that," Mrs. Macken said, looking him in the eye. Mr. Bywater laughed easily.

"Well, actually, I came to see your boy. Is he about? I told him four-thirty." He checked his watch. Mrs. Macken nodded.

"I'll get him for you." She walked into the storeroom and came out with Cass behind her. Cass felt a knot of excitement in the pit of his stomach. It wouldn't be long now.

"Would you like to come up, Mr. Bywater? Can you manage . . . ?"

"Sure thing. I'm O.K. Lead the way." He jerked his head at Trevor, who broke off his conversation with Alanna Caterina and followed them. O'Mara had slipped into the shop with a group of children and waited now behind the shelves near the stairs.

"Would you like to sit down?" asked Cass politely, waving a vague hand at the chairs in the sitting room.

"Oh, I don't think that'll be necessary, thanks. Just get the key ring and I'll be going."

"It's on the roof," Cass said, feeling foolish. "I've got to go out my bedroom window." Mr. Bywater laughed.

"You're a cool customer!" He looked round the room. "We'll go into your room then, O.K.?" Mr. Bywater followed Cass right inside, but Trevor stayed near the door. Cass was working his way across the iron to the parapet and did not see O'Mara push past Trevor.

"Watch it!" Trevor growled. O'Mara ignored him. He was looking at Mr. Bywater with hungry eyes.

"It's stuck tight," called Cass, trying to get the tennis ball loose. In the end it had to be cut open. He climbed back in through the window and handed the key ring to its owner.

"Thanks, son. Thanks a lot." Mr. Bywater took it, threw it up ino the air, caught it and was about to pocket it but swung round when O'Mara hissed his frustration.

There was still no matchbox!

O'Mara didn't care any more about disguises. His eyes burned into Bywater's and the man seemed unable to move.

Trevor broke the silence. "I thought the formula was here. . . ."

"That's right. You can have it—for the right money." Mr. Bywater spoke with an effort. He still had his eyes locked on O'Mara's.

"I might just raise Trevor's bid." Trevor swung round. It was Adam.

"Come off it, Adam. What would you do with it?"

"Give it back to its owners, perhaps," said Adam lazily. "Are you bidding too, O'Mara?" O'Mara took no notice.

Mr. Bywater began to sweat. His hands trembled. Slowly he grasped the brass button and twisted it. The top unscrewed and in the hollow was a microdot protected by tape and an object the size of a penny, slightly convex, heavy, smooth, opaque. O'Mara hissed again, eyes fastened on the ank. "What on earth's that?" Adam asked. Mr. Bywater recovered himself. He flipped the disc out through the window.

"Nothing important," he said. "This is what you're after." He tapped the microdot. "Now, gentlemen . . . ."

As the ank hit the iron and began to roll, O'Mara leaped for the window, but Seville got to it first, chasing the disc into the gutter. He arched his back and spat at O'Mara, who retreated. "Get it!" he commanded, coming back. He was shaking. "Get it away from that cat!"

"Don't be in such a hurry," protested Cass. "It doesn't belong to you, it belongs to Mr. Bywater." As he spoke, Cass was trying to remember where he'd seen the disc before. Had he actually seen it, or was it a picture? He couldn't remember.

O'Mara was trembling. He seemed to be shrinking. His face was twisted with anger and hate and, yes, fear. Cass looked at him in astonishment. "It's mine. It was never Bywater's. Always mine. YOU WILL GET IT NOW!" He was too ridiculous. Cass laughed.

"I'll get it for you, O'Mara. It's only a cat, nothing to be scared of." Trevor started to cross the room. Cass slammed the window down and stood in front of it.

"No you don't!"

"You shut up!" Trevor spoke roughly. There was a funny sound from the doorway. It was Clare, barefooted, in her dressing gown. She was staring at Trevor, white faced, horror in her eyes.

"It was YOU!" she said, pointing at Trevor. "It was you took me from Vincent! You had a stocking on your face.

You said 'Shut up!' and put a needle in my arm!" Trevor laughed.

"You'll never prove it, Clare. Never. Anyway, you're O.K., so why worry?" He laughed again. "Vincent was the one . . . ."

Clare ran across the room to Cass. "Make him go away, Mack. Please make him . . . ."

"It's all right, sweetheart. He's going right now." Mr. Macken came into the room, his face white with fury, hands clenched. Beside him was the detective who had been in charge of the search for Clare. Trevor looked as if he might try to make a bolt for it, but there were too many people in the room.

As he comforted Clare, Cass was vaguely aware of Adam telling Mr. Bywater he had the wrong microdot, that some guy named Darren Pryse had picked up the wrong one and he didn't have the formula at all. Mr. Bywater bellowed like a wounded bull and charged out of the room and down the stairs.

"Look after Clare, Stewart," called their father as he and Adam went in pursuit.

O'Mara was almost done. The anger and fear and frustration had sapped his small remaining power. He seemed translucent and was getting smaller and smaller. Cass hesitated. Clare nodded at him. "Get it," she mouthed. Without wanting to do it, she was inside O'Mara's mind. It was terrified of becoming human, of not being able to leave the Earth. Clare knew that he could no longer command her; the power was gone.

Cass opened the window and climbed out. Seville was still crouching in the gutter, the small disc between his front paws.

He got up mewing when Cass approached and rubbed his head against the boy's legs. Cass picked up the ank, marveling at its perfection, and brought it back to the window. He handed it to Clare.

O'Mara seemed all eyes. They burned, then dulled. Clare had his ank. Clare, who with her brother, had pitted her puny human mind against his. Clare whom he had shut up, starved, harassed, left to be burned. She held his fate in her hand. Thakover was upon him. He fought off the inevitable moment of change, of becoming the substance of the long illusion.

Clare did not speak. She squatted on her heels in front of O'Mara and held out the ank on the flat of her hand. O'Mara took a step forward, lips drawn back, wary. When he reached for the ank, Clare's fingers curled a little as if they were about to close. This small, desperate, unearthly creature with a cringing mind, was this her tormentor, jailer? She knew he could no longer harm her, but his closeness made her flesh creep. With a sigh of conscious effort, she straightened her fingers. The ank winked on the palm of her hand. Like giving sugar to a horse, Cass thought, watching with held breath. O'Mara took it slowly, letting his fingers rest for a moment on Clare's hand, then, with a tearing cry, he pushed the ank into place and, leaving O'Mara behind him, zapped through the open window and away over the rooftops. Clare and Cass leaned together on the windowsill and watched until he was out of sight.

"Poor little feller," said Clare.

Mr. Bywater, running toward the car, tripped and fell. Mrs. Leadbetter was in Vichelli's buying vegetables. "I'm coming!" she shrieked. "Don't worry. I got me St. John's. . . ."

Adam and Mr. Macken came back to the shop laughing. Alanna Caterina raised an eyebrow at them. Adam stayed to talk to her. There was so much they had to say to each other.

A few days later, Peter Graham and Cass were with Father O'Donovan in his study. Peter had made the tea and Cass was exploring the *Bait* tin. "What sort of bait is this, Father?" Cass called out. "Tastes a bit odd, doesn't it?"

Father O'Donovan groaned. "It's a judgment on me for having a proud stomach, me boy. I don't know what's happened to Mrs. Leadbetter's cooking. She's using up some horrible stuff she bought a lot of. . . . I don't know how she could have done it, but I'm suffering, I'm suffering. Could you hold your nose while you eat and pretend it's delicious? No? Neither can I! But it's that or nothing. She won't cook me any more until it's used up."

Peter Graham produced a packet from his pocket. "Would chocolate biscuits do?" he asked. "I just happened to buy them on the way round."

"Praise God! Don't worry about a plate, Cassowary, we'll eat out of the packet and there won't be any left to put away. Pour the tea, there's a good lad, and start from the beginning. I want to hear everything, now. . . ."

Cass nursed his mug of tea and swallowed the remains of a chocolate biscuit. "Well," he began, "see, there was this man running. . . ."